INDISCREET MEMOIRS

She rested one rounded knee upon a chair, thus emphasising the beautifully shaped line of her thigh. Then she tugged slowly at the hem of the silk slip and pulled it upwards with exasperating deliberation as if hestitating. I heard someone beside me gasp and I turned round. No one there. It was my own breathing I had heard, a strange, unfamiliar and disturbing sound . . . she raised the flimsy veil above her breasts. In this frankly perverse pose she was offering herself to my gaze with complete innocence and a cool smile . . .

Also available

INDISCREET MEMOIRS

Alain Dorval

NEXUS

A Nexus Book
Published in 1985
by the Paperback Division of
W.H. Allen & Co. Plc
Sekforde House, 175/9 St. John Street
London EC1V 4LL

Reprinted 1989

First published in France as
Souvenirs Indiscrets D'Un Voleur D'Images
First published in Great Britain by
W. H. Allen & Co. Plc 1984

Copyright © Le Sycomore 1983
Translation copyright © W. H. Allen 1984

Printed and bound in Great Britain by
Courier International Ltd, Tiptree, Essex

ISBN 0 352 31516 4

INDISCREET
MEMOIRS

I was very surprised to find Yves Morhant at my door. I had been summoned reluctantly by an inopportune ring on the bell.

'This is a bit off your beat, isn't it?' I asked him.

'I'm moving soon to the Right Bank,' he replied.

'What can I do for you?'

'I came to give you this stuff so you can go on being my ghostwriter.'

He then entrusted me with everything: unfinished notebooks, little memo-pads containing scribbled notes and phrases, some rough drafts, a few scattered pages of manuscript and, rather curiously, two recordings. On these his voice, always so attractive to women, spouted conceitedly, reciting pieces of poetry and assorted fragments of autobiography. An odd mixture.

'I assume that, as usual, I won't be paid any too well.'

'A sort of token of our continuing hostility, if you like . . .'

1

'There I feel we've already collaborated: as far as that goes, you've certainly cashed in.'

'I'll let you put your own name to the book, or whatever pseudonym you may choose to adopt.'

'Will you be its hero?'

'That's up to you. I know you are devious enough to disabuse me of that particular notion.'

'I accept. Literature is worth a Black Mass. Would you like a hundred francs towards a sandwich in the corner *bistro*? I can't very well offer you a meal here.'

'No thanks. They're waiting for me at the Grand Véfour.'

He left then and I listened expectantly as he descended the ramshackle staircase. But he didn't come to grief. I heard no violent squeal of brakes, no slam of metal into flesh, no noise of a car-crash at all. It only remained for me to wish him severe indigestion. That too was an unlikely conjecture, for he was something to do with the Michelin Guides and on friendly terms with most of the main restaurateurs in France.

Once again I had given in, for the sake of shared school-days during which our mutual dislike had been both cordial and extensive. Morhant had always had the best of the bargain since he was a handsome boy from a well-to-do family. He was also clever enough to be charming and not too smug. My own background was far less grand and over my threadbare collar the acne used to erupt.

Yet I had accepted – because Yves Morhant does not fascinate me: he is neither my worst enemy nor some ideal projection of myself. He is my antithesis, someone of whom I disapprove but needs must describe in order to assert myself. At any rate, as a character he is not without interest.

My desire wings towards the gate of Dream. For me, moving in a world of concealed images is vitally important.

I am old now. If I have amused myself by cataloguing my sexual discoveries and my real, imagined or half-glimpsed loves, it is from the need to find self-realisation, to fill the gaps, directing myself in the impossible film, the ultimate adventure. As I conceive it, such an adventure is absolute in the sense that now it is ideal and well-assembled – or even artfully disorganised – and above all, completely to my liking.

Y.M.

The deities of the spring tides
Let their tresses flow
Pursuing you must go
After that lovely shade you seek

APOLLINAIRE

1

The house had been warmly recommended to me. It stood in its own rather rambling grounds, beside a small river, and I liked the look of it immediately.

I was in fact born in a house surrounded by luxuriantly overgrown parkland, but I have never felt at ease with nature. I wanted nature's cocoon around my own home so that I could feel more insulated, secure. Heavy tapestries, felt-backed pile carpets, the secret nooks and crannies and hiding-places common to large, half-empty houses, were all sensually indispensable where I was concerned – so were attics, crisply lit yet dark enough under the stars, or murky cellars full of ghosts. I was the furtive one, the watchful eye, the taker of pictures. A voyeur. I needed to look before I took.

Madame introduced all her young ladies. They were either vivacious, goodlooking or sexually desirable one way or another. I had not been misled: that pleased me.

She invited me to a lavish dinner.

'What do you like best?' she enquired, no doubt referring to my erotic preferences.

'Dream', I said.

She gazed at me in astonishment.

'And my instruments are in there,' I added, pointing to a large suitcase I'd placed in one corner of the room.

She grew startled.

'My girls don't much go in for being knocked about, Monsieur, and . . .'

'Don't worry. That suitcase merely contains three cameras, tripods and photographic plates. I want to relive some real or imaginary adventures, created by photographs. Leave me to soak up the atmosphere for a while, then I shall select from your girls according to their powers of evocation.'

Reassured by this, she agreed.

Pleasure in the forbidden. My mother had married a rich bourgeois, whose son I doubtless was. She entertained a great deal. Two ladies, or rather a married woman and a young girl, used to ply me with kisses, bonbons and all sorts of playful attentions. Their names were Mme Edmée Chartier, the local vet's wife, and Mlle Thérèse Janvier, daughter of the Mayor, who was also one of the town's main hoteliers. My feelings for them were of gratitude, pure and simple. One day, however, I returned somewhat unexpectedly to that rather mysterious and inviting place where my mother would serve tea. My uncle, my father's brother who was then a bachelor, was sprawled in an armchair facing the pair of them. They were seated on some cushions, smoking, and with their skirts tucked up. Their postures seemed to me distinctly bizarre and scarcely in keeping with the notion I had maintained of their due dignity. They were displaying their legs, the sight of which affected me only through its suddenness and incongruity. Indeed, I was shocked mainly by the relaxed, even careless appearance of these two well-liked and familiar people.

This memory haunted me long afterwards. About three years later, when sexual stirrings afflicted me for the first time, that tableau assumed for me its full erotic significance. Thus pleasure in the forbidden and my own eroticism, which inclined towards a taste for secrecy and the fleeting glimpse, gradually established themselves. To complete this first set of snapshots, I discovered in my uncle's private den, the attic, a photograph of these two ladies – taken in that very same drawing-room – and in which, wearing identical hats but opulently nude, both were concealing their silken mysteries behind their handbags. (I took pleasure thereafter in stroking these handbags, fantasising deliciously about what each had concealed.) This photograph gave me an almost constant erection for several days on end, and I tried to satisfy myself in those special secret corners of my domain, situated in cellars and lofts.

To prolong the dialogue, to extend the vision itself and its actual picture – these were my drugs. Hidden inside a corner-cupboard in the attic, I overheard my uncle talking to a young man who was the son of the biggest landowner in the district. My uncle was showing him some of his own paintings and drawings. They soon got on to the subject of women.

'Do you know Thérèse Janvier well? I believe she comes round here quite often.'

'All too well!' my uncle replied.

'You mean you . . .? I thought Thérèse was supposed to be so reserved?'

'She's as easy to poke as any little whore. Listen, when I was invited to the Janviers', I was offered a rather unexpected dessert. You know old father Janvier, he of the grotesque moustache and prosperous paunch? Those self-satisfied grocer's airs and graces of his! Well, after the meal, simply from a desire to do something perverse, under the very roof of an arch-bourgeois like himself, I gave Thérèse a sign, and then went out, with the excuse that I felt like going for a breather on my own. I waited for her and when she emerged I thrust her into a small drawing-room. I knew that apart from myself no one would be unconventional enough to leave the table and forgo the post-prandial fug, nor the cognac and the pompous reek of our good Mayor's truncheon of a cigar. There is always some slight risk, however. Anyhow, I did give my Thérèse a tumble. I installed her on a piece of furniture of the required height and took my time gazing at her gashed desire whose outline was clearly visible in relief under her drawers. One jet-black tuft had managed to escape constraint and when I unveiled the whole mane it bristled crisply against my palm. My middle finger penetrated its centre and Thérèse moaned. I fluttered and probed until her entire body seemed to spill open, her eyes rolled upward and her mouth framed unuttered if not unutterable obscenities. Then I saw her remove the undergarment in question and wipe herself with it before concealing it under the sideboard and returning to the drawing-room. You can well imagine that all that afternoon I had plenty of occasion to slide my hand swiftly and stealthily beneath her skirt to gauge the humid, rustling sweetness of her dulcet cleft.'

'But had you had her before that?'

'On numerous occasions. I remember our first carnal bout. I was stretched out on a chaise longue upon the terrace. The weather was exceedingly hot. My sister, brother-in-law, Mme Chartier and her husband, and Thérèse too, had all gone for a stroll in the grounds. It became increasingly sultry, heavy, and then the storm broke. For some reason Thérèse came back, running. She was already absolutely soaked. She told me that the others had probably taken shelter in the small dovecote that now served as a shed. I advised her to take off her clothes and dry them out. She entered the bedroom to do as I suggested, but I picked the right moment to interrupt her there, just as she stepped out of her petticoat. Her knickers had already been abandoned. She shivered slightly, offering me a fine rear view: her rump was full as an autumn moon, rounded and juicy as a stolen peach. She wanted to get dressed again quickly and was nervous about being surprised, but I proved an admiring lunar explorer, my tongue delving intrepidly into that deep ravine which split the moon in half, and ransacking that divide until I touched upon the savoury eyelet, tasting its rosy delights. How delicious the child was! If you'll pardon the expression, buggery was fine with her.'

'It can't be true . . . Well, old man, that really takes the cake!'

'Quite. A rich spicy one at that, you might say, a hole to digest you whole.'

'Little shy Thérèse . . .'

'Blushing bright red in her confusion, her bum in the air, old chap. Terrified of being caught in the act, yet playing a devilishly neat jig upon my virility. She was by no means a virgin.'

This overheard conversation soon inflamed my curiosity. Gently insidious, then violent or outrageously abandoned images replaced the freshfaced portrait of my favourite bestower of bonbons. And so, more and more, my erotic sensibility was being shaped.

I made a veritable epic out of what had happened between Thérèse and my uncle, projecting on the screen of my mind a succession of bedroom orgies, trying to guess Mlle Janvier's previous lovers and who had initiated her or to envisage the role Mme Chartier might have played in these excesses. And much else besides . . .

'Every pleasure the hand can provide' was for me an already reliable and sometimes perfect enjoyment. My hand, reaching its objective, would revel in and palp the present, but by then no past remained, only an uncertain future. Whereas the image before my eyes, which I had imagined, would send me into a drowsy ecstasy, finding its precise place or counterpart, however diverse, in a book or a film that was to become ever more specific as the days wore on.

That is why it was well over twenty years later before I had the opportunity of possessing Thérèse Janvier. Alma, that ingenuous inmate of the brothel, gave me the chance by acting out the part of Thérèse, which she did to perfection. An unusually solemn-looking girl with a hint of the Creole, she appeared with her moonlike buttocks suggestively veiled, and she too knew how to satisfy one by the narrower route, wriggling in an abstracted way that both entranced and excited. She seemed preoccupied, absorbed by some perpetual and deeply private daydream while I visited Sodom, drawn in her restless wake.

Those days I was something of a little aristocrat and was very keen on the harpsichord. I had a pleasant if somewhat aloof cousin of twelve who used to practise hard: she seemed eager to turn into Rameau's niece! I forgave her that because of her fetching and reassuring pigtails. When I was invited to come along for one of those keyboard evenings in the family mansion I would follow the rhythms of those pigtails far more enthusiastically than the wrong notes their owner purveyed.

The chateau was in the Auvergne, a moss-covered house in the middle of a sloping meadow dotted with enormous chestnut trees. In the distance, the hills melted into mystery, but it was the vast, rather rustic building itself I liked best.

The parents of my pigtailed paragon entertained frequently. Her elder sister Nadine, a striking brunette – more of whom later – had invited down a German girlfriend. The latter was blonde as a Valkyrie and played the harpsichord divinely: she made me think of the great Bavarian forests, of their fantastic castles with a myriad rooms and as many secrets hazily reflected in the calm blue waters of the lakes.

On the third night of my stay I could not sleep and, plucking up my courage, decided to do some exploring. As I set off, material rustled, furniture cracked – as if transmitting messages. I glided around like the proverbial ship in the night. At the foot of the staircase a gleam of light caught my eye. I thought at once of burglars, but the hushed murmur of female voices proved I was mistaken. I descended, my feet sinking into the heavy stair-carpet. When I had stealthily reached the end of the left-hand corridor I could see into the library.

Once again – I was now just thirteen years old – the scene I saw shocked me more by its incongruous nature, since I knew those involved, than by its delectable eroticism. I soon regained my composure, however. After a momentary speculation as to whether or not I could be mistaken, I did decide to believe my eyes and sought only to enjoy the spectacle to the full.

Two contrasting naked forms, fair and dark, were blithely engaged in reading each other the amorous exploits of a juvenile Don Juan of the Belle Epoque. To do this they must have agreed upon a nocturnal expedition, stealing the library key in order to ferret among the secret drawers. The mere thought of this conspiracy to get up to mischief increased my excitement all the more. I was the voyeur keeping a peeping eye on two voyeuses. Such a situation increased threefold the power of the image itself – which in this case was not invented. They were standing, and their sumptuous rumps seemed twins. I was, too, delighted by their slender thighs. I sensed in both of them such a feverish complicity, expressed by various stifled gasps and giggles, so keen a desire for the book never to end – together with such avid haste in reading it that they had already almost reached the conclusion. I could therefore guess all too well what would follow when they returned to the room they were sharing. I myself had two good reasons for pushing back quickly into my own: to avoid being caught and to indulge in some necessary manual relief.

What should I reveal next? My attempt to seduce a young maidservant, and the attempted seduction of myself by a lady I have not yet named but whom I have mentioned indirectly: Mme Louise d'Evremont, the mother of my pigtailed playmate.

I was then aged sixteen and fairly aware from appreciative female glances that women found me handsome enough. What was more, I had plenty of pocket money and a good future ahead of me.

Mme Louise d'Evremont was a kind, friendly woman of forty. At that time I too had my own special den in our attic: there I used to paint or idle away the hours. That particular day the house was empty. I heard somebody calling from the ground floor, so I leaned out of the bull's-eye window and shouted down that I was the only one at home, up in the attic. Soon I heard the stair creak, the door was pushed open and a smiling Mme d'Evremont appeared.

'Well Monsieur Yves, no one exactly rushes around in your house. I was counting on being put up here for a while.'

She always used to smile at me, but just then I sensed that something was going to happen.

'I adore attics,' she went on. 'But it's hot in here. Wouldn't you like a model?'

She lay full-length on some scattered cushions and adopted something of an indecent posture, thus enabling me to study a pair of rounded, indeed plump, thighs, whose whiteness was accentuated by the shadow and her dark stockings. Her sex, along with the fundamental furrow, were concealed by tight embroidered knickers. She looked as if she were offering me an invitation.

'Is that a little naughty perhaps?' she remarked.

Yet this older woman offering herself did not seduce me there and then. Despite the fact that the attic surroundings were ideal for such activities, despite her own attractions – and she resembled some character from Sade or Restif de la Bretonne – I looked away in embarrassment.

She rearranged her dress and rose to her feet.

'You're a fool,' she said almost with annoyance.

Then she went downstairs again.

My lust was only roused that night, in fantasy, when I recalled the creamy opulence of her plump thighs, which so ripely enclosed an experienced sex.

* * *

With the little serving-maid it was quite different. What memories! Even now the mind falters in the recollection. We had a sizeable domestic staff. Our cook was devoted to us. She was an old, or rather elderly, woman from the provinces, and from her native Périgord she supplied us with a pretty little Aquitaine girl I found thoroughly intimidating. She was the cook's niece. At sixteen she had a twinkle in her eye and sometimes a sort of mildly cheeky quality due more to naivety than boldness. Even my stern architect father was enchanted by her. (Although I don't think my father ever had an extramarital affair.) Luckily for me, my uncle was then finally doing his deferred military service: thus he was in no position to lead her astray. Anyhow, my father was very strict and would not have countenanced any fun and games with the domestics. Though a stern enough employer, he did pay well. Our servants proved anxious to keep their jobs and all were keen without obsequiousness: my father saw to that. Thanks to or because of him my uncle had to restrain his urges to seduce servants and chambermaids.

As I remarked earlier, Cécile intimidated me. I sensed only too well that she was interested in me. One morning I found myself alone again, with everyone in the family and the household either out or away for one reason or another. That occasionally happened and was something

I quite welcomed, for the whole house was then completely mine. I had realised this while I was getting dressed, and when I was ready I embarked upon a private exploratory tour. My taste for the forbidden guided me. As I tried to open my mother's bedroom door I felt some slight resistance. I pushed until the armchair blocking it rolled aside. I went in and was astonished by what I saw. It was quite a spectacle: Cécile stood in front of the wardrobe mirror, clad only in her underwear. She was staring at me in acute anguish. I had heard her little cry of fright. Then I understood: what most embarrassed her was not so much being surprised in a state of undress, but being discovered trying on lingerie that did not belong to her. Things suddenly began to make sense: while cleaning my mother's room Cécile had been attracted by the slips and petticoats hanging in the wardrobe and could not resist trying one on, playing the lady of the manor. She knew its owner was absent: the armchair against the door was placed there only to warn her of the possible arrival of another servant. Although this was now clear to me, I adopted a calculatedly haughty tone.

'Are you stealing, Cécile?'

'Monsieur Yves, I swear I was only trying it on . . . I promise you!'

That I well knew, and I was incapable of prolonging her agony, but I pressed home my cowardly advantage.

'That's as may be,' I told her, 'but I should

17

like to know what you are wearing under that garment.'

'I'm quite naked sir,' she said with a faint smile which mingled shyness and mischief – for she had suddenly realised what was in the wind.

'Off with it then, because I don't believe you.'

'I daren't.'

'Do you wish me to inform my mother of your misbehaviour?'

She seemed to be making a decision – her resolve influenced, however, by something other than fear of denunciation. She rested one rounded knee upon a chair, thus emphasising the beautifully shaped line of her thigh. Then she tugged slowly at the hem of the silk slip and pulled it upwards with exasperating deliberation as if hesitating. I heard someone beside me gasp and I turned round. No one there. It was my own breathing I had heard, a strange, unfamiliar and disturbing sound . . .

She raised the flimsy veil above her breasts. In this frankly perverse pose she was offering herself to my gaze with complete innocence and a cool smile.

I was stunned. This young girl's calm beauty did not merely arouse me sexually but somehow affected my entire consciousness: it was as if my sexuality were twin to my soul. Although remaining motionless, without reaction or any real desire to make a move, I had a raging urge to possess this adolescent utterly, to absorb her in my very being, to feel her presence within

18

my deepest self. For some time I stayed dumbstruck, contemplating her wide hips and those delicate yet sturdy loins which would one day make her an ideal mother. I stared at her small, round, pink-crowned breasts; at that enchanting tiny dimple, her navel; gazing finally upon her soft, sparse fleece.

At last I moved closer, fascinated. I fell upon my knees and plunged my face into her fine downy mount then, laughing and crying simultaneously, I assailed it with kisses, lip-play and flickers of the tongue. I was at once glutton and worshipper at the shrine of a voluptuous faith, anxiously yet humbly awaiting the wafer. And I stammered: 'Cécile, oh Cécile! . . . My love . . .'

Desire drove me and I had the impulse to hurl her onto my mother's bed. To do this seemed a sort of sacrilege just then, but the iconoclastic aspect of such an act stimulated me. I undid my fly buttons and when her inexpert fingers touched my swollen pride she trembled and uttered a little gasp, which endeared her to me all the more. Her thighs parted, exposing a mossy paradise which happened to be jet-black and pink.

Our virginities melted away in the sweet, oppressive ardour of our newfound, beginners' passion.

Cécile was truly my first full, purely sexual experience – and I use 'purely' in all senses of the word. Now as you will see, and have already seen, by then I had been initiated into certain perverse experiences more to do with fondling or, to be frank, with masturbation, than with any real amorous bout. Into this category of voluptuous or tantalizing discoveries I must place an adventure I had had concerning a lady mentioned earlier.

The riddle of the lewd photograph of Mlle Janvier and Mme Chartier that I had found troubled my early adolescent nights. I had to wait until I was fifteen, and for one spring afternoon in particular, before I tried something which even in hindsight seems idiotic.

Mme Chartier had been invited to dinner. After the meal her husband and my father went through to the smoking-room; she and my mother descended into the garden. I followed them, concealing myself as best I could. They were conversing very animatedly. I kept thinking how this lady, so beautiful and proper, had allowed herself to be photographed in the nude together with another young woman of good family in a highly questionable if appropriately artistic pose – by someone obviously not her husband and who certainly was my uncle.

She and my mother were fond of roses and my mother left to find a pair of secateurs, in order to cut her a few. I then approached her discreetly. When she saw me she gave a pleasant wave.

'Ah, Yves, are you coming to admire the roses, too?'

'Oh no,' I retorted cynically.

Whereupon I promptly produced the photograph of herself and Mlle Janvier in the buff. She started, blushed, but then regained her composure.

'What now? Where did you get that?'

'I stole it. . . . This is what I want you to do: make an excuse, say you need to pee for instance' (I certainly intended a smutty innuendo here) 'and then head for my room.'

She agreed. Then my mother returned and I went back to my room. After a short while someone tapped lightly at the door. I opened it and she entered furtively.

'What is it you want, then?'

'Could you show me everything, like the photograph but without the handbag?'

'Fool!' she said with what was almost a scornful shrug.

Making the most of my newly-acquired adolescent strength and hot as a cockerel, I leaped at her and she fell to the floor. I flung myself upon her and assailed her brazenly if clumsily. Still holding in one hand a rose my mother had given her, she flailed at me with it and its stem scratched me slightly. That I clearly remember, for it is not every day that one gets whipped by a flower. I caught glimpses of her flesh: her breasts (dare I call them heaving?) were escaping from her half-open dress and this added the requisite note of violated fragility. She pushed me off and I did not try to press home my advantage. But as I leaned back I could relish a picture which even today I find overwhelming

21

when I recollect it. Amid a seething mass of lace and crumpled silks her thighs were visible, and her buttocks too, whose cleft was masked by a wisp of split knickers. I must confess that in the sheer ardour of the attempted rape my trembling hand had managed to touch that soft, humid hairy area which the flimsy piece of material concealed: this was what had made her gasp her order to me to desist. I had more or less obeyed, though by feasting my eyes upon the spectacle of her shamefaced confusion and cowed femininity, I had in a way 'possessed' her.

This vision of her, then, was both affecting and symbolic. Here was the neatly attired lady, respectable conformist bored with her Sunday best. That thrashing rose she held in her gloved hand perhaps bore some similarity to the nipple so summarily uncovered and which a hand had palped; it might equally well symbolize the very thing the frothy lace was masking, that other, nether rose. The gloved hand, also, suggested something to me which I did not then know how to interpret: in that attitude Mme Chartier became for me the symbol of elegant sodomy, of gentle flagellation. She was both slave and mistress, submissive yet dominantly perverse, fashionably clad yet capable of being had, tumbled like any little peasant girl . . .

She stood up again, trying to restore some semblance of order amid her sartorial and psychic confusion.

'What a little brute you are . . . A handsome

little brute. We'll meet again,' she announced prophetically.

Some time later I met her again one Sunday morning, coming out of Mass. It was I who felt most shame.

'Monsieur Yves Morhant . . .'

As she called my name she beckoned to me. She looked if anything amused, even ironic, but not in the least angry.

'So one doesn't say hello to one's mother's friends any more. What a naughty lad!'

'. . . I didn't expect to speak to you . . .'

'My goodness, he didn't expect to speak to me. Well, anyhow will you see me home? We can go a rather pleasant way, the road has lilacs either side.'

I took this to be ragging rather than invitation. No doubt she intended giving me a lecture or challenging me in some manner.

I was mistaken. By choosing the small path behind the church, the one leading through some fields to a group of five substantial houses, she had a very specific purpose in mind.

Halfway along this path she stopped to rummage inside her handbag. She found some object which she kept hidden from me while she was talking.

'You know, my dear Yves, that I was weak-willed enough to let myself be photographed – with Mlle Janvier – in a rather unseemly pose, I do admit. Also, since you exploited that error of mine in a way you no doubt recall, I insist on showing you somebody you know well . . . very well, even, in a photograph just as private, taken in the same place and by the same person.'

I must have turned very pale. Indeed, I immediately thought she was referring to my mother, although that idea did seem quite crazy.

She finally passed me the photograph. I took a deep breath and at the same time experienced a shock which almost stopped my heartbeat: then, simultaneously also, the blood rushed to my loins, concentrating upon and pumping into that organ which it forced to firm and throbbing attention.

To introduce an element of suspense at this point, I shall indulge in some genealogy. My mother was the daughter of a solicitor aptly named Bourgeois. He had three daughters for all of whom he arranged good marriages – thus using his numerous and influential professional contacts to considerable effect.

Suzanne the eldest was five years older than the youngest girl, and married a fat linen manufacturer. Edwige, three years my mother's senior, received as her dutifully paternal gift an army colonel for a husband – a patrician land-owner, in the bargain, which was all to the good. For me the most interesting thing about this handsome military man was his name, Jean de Brissac. My mother, Jeanne Bourgeois, the youngest child, became Jeanne Morhant, architect's wife. Suzanne was childless and I was the only child. The Brissacs alone had more than one child: a son, Rodolphe, one year older than myself, and Claire their daughter, three years younger than I. It was Jean de Brissac's cousin, Laurent d'Evremont, who was father to my sweet little pigtailed girlfriend.

I was therefore stupefied to see this lurid photograph of one of my aunts, and what was more, of the very one who seemed the most unapproachable, remote and in so far as anything erotic was concerned, even frigid. It was Suzanne, the wealthy industralist's wife, she who was always swathed in furs, and whom I could scarcely envisage engaged in bedroom frolics. But human beings all have their hidden side.

Suzanne was no longer in the first flush of youth, but the photograph certainly caught the eye. She was to be seen in her brassière, wearing stockings and expensive high-heeled shoes, but it was her corset that was most remarkable, tightly constricting her plump bourgeois stomach. She had fleshy thighs and huge buttocks, yet I found myself thoroughly aroused. What were the components of my excitement? The fact that this mature if not overblown lady invariably gave the impression of prudery. The fact that I knew her well, and that here she was now revealing herself to me, despite herself, and beyond any deceitful social veneer of keeping up appearances. There were many other factors too, all contributing to my confused state of excitement. My mother's elder sister had been photographed in her underwear by my father's younger brother. Most of all, above all else, I seemed to see in her, although she had aged and run to fat, something of my own mother, for Jeanne closely resembled her sister.

'You're disgusting,' I said to Edmée Chartier.

'No more so than you, my dear!'

And then I felt her hand move rapidly to and fro, over the front of my trousers.

'Well well,' she said, 'you're hardly very proper yourself when it comes to a fullscale portrait of your aunt.'

Her expert fingers unbuttoned, invaded and gripped. She drew out my stiffened prick and in that moment I became aware of the scent of lilac all around us. When the tugging motions were under way I found myself overcome by the paroxysm of an ejaculation both magical and sensual. At that moment I was loath to let Mme Chartier see me so young, so childishly clumsy. But despite everything I let myself be drawn to orgasm by that beige kid-gloved hand, while staring at the photograph which blurred, swayed and made incestuous advances to me. I then had an insight into the not wholly grasped significance of the gloved female hand – symbol of the elegant and (as it were) underhand masturbatrix. My belly jerked forward and from my reddened penis there pulsed seething jets of a whitish liquid. I groaned loudly and shut my eyes. Opening them again I vaguely discerned my teacher's face and gouts of that thick, syrupy trickling substance, white against the lilac, oozing down a sprig of those mauve blossoms. It seemed that with Mme Chartier I was doomed to flowers.

In my adolescent naivety, my youthful male stupidity, I imagined that I had won Mme Chartier. This was not the case. Without actually avoiding me, she put me in my place, and I came to see that what had transpired on that memorable Sunday morning had been a subtle form of revenge. So that I would almost believe it to be a surrender.

Seven or eight months later the Chartiers moved from the district.

The narrative of these early experiences would be incomplete without the inclusion of a misadventure I had – this in my own beloved region, along the banks of the Loire. We used to live outside the town, a good two kilometres away. At that particular time during my adolescence I would often go down to the river alone, for I was tormented by the lusts of the flesh and a desire for potentially pleasant encounters. I would follow a footpath, take a roundabout route or the most direct one. I'd stroll along daydreaming, but I was on the look-out too, trying to fuel my fantasies. These would be satisfied by a pair of bourgeois buttocks tightly slung in fine silk, or with a bold and buxom bosom half-bared during some ripely bucolic occupation.

I would sometimes meet up with a thoroughly disreputable youth of my own age, his yellowish hair already thinning and his general demeanour downright unprepossessing. Indeed, his greyish complexion and its very texture resembled lumpy porridge. He was ugly, poor and criminal. I was rather scared of him, for he seemed to set no store by my appearance or my parents' status in the community. He did not even suspect that one could defer to the sort of young gentleman I was. Quite the contrary. When he happened to pass me he would spit in my direction, as though inadvertently, or toss a rotten apple at my feet so that it would burst into bits, soiling my trouser legs. To achieve a similar effect, perhaps a stone might be deftly lobbed into a muddy puddle.

One day he accosted me, verbally grabbed my lapels, so to speak, while he sat nonchalantly on a gate.

'Hey, you!'

His accent was not local. It was said that his father, formerly a labourer, had lived in or near Paris and had gravitated to working on the land, after casual employment helping out market-gardeners in Argenteuil. Also, that his decision to come out to the provinces was not entirely voluntary, being taken upon his release from prison. Everyone in the area was convinced he had done time. The mother was apparently Egyptian, a grubby-looking houri and a laundress, self-styled. They had lived in the neighbourhood for two or three years, adding daily to their bad and richly deserved reputation.

I tried to ignore this potential jailbird and continued on my way. But he leaped down agilely to confront me, blocking my path.

'Yeah, you. Talking to you. Listen, sell you my sister.'

I gazed at him in amazement then, trying hard to match his revolting, basilisk stare.

'Let me pass.'

'Sell you my sister, honest. You can't lose.'

The cream of the jest was that I knew the sister by sight. A timid, scrawny-bodied little creature, unkempt and always dirty, if slightly cleaner than her brother. She had ginger, or to be more accurate, reddish-brown hair, but there was something about her pale green eyes. Out of pride, and also perhaps because I was somewhat disconcerted, I asked him:

'Will it cost much?'

'Ten francs.'

The sum seemed excessive to me. But I did have some reserve pocket money and I knew I could filch some non-returnable loans from my parents' pockets and purses. Not real thieving, borrowing out of necessity.

'Ten francs,' he went on, 'and she'll let you see the lot. You can go the whole way too.'

These final words made me blush, for he had stressed 'whole' in a subtler, sleazier way than one might imagine. I'd already seen the lot, or almost the lot. But I hadn't ever gone the whole way.

'Where would this be?'

'Don't you worry. I know one of those islands in the middle of the Loire. Safe as anything. I'll row you across and take you back after.'

'And what if you robbed me?'

'You're pretty sharp, you are. I'm on the level. Hundred sous, then, in advance. Hundred when we get back. Sis'll be smartly togged out.'

'When?'

'Tomorrow afternoon.'

As I was hesitating, he added:

'You'll know all about girls then. Eh, stupid?'

'I don't need to. I know already.'

He looked me up and down, calculatingly, then remarked with some disgust: 'Oh, so it's true that you toffs . . .'

Then, spitting copiously, he stood aside. I left without answering him. I even worried lest he resume the offensive, but out of the corner of my eye – for I dared not turn round – I saw him sitting on his gate again.

From then on, however, I became almost delirious. Already I no longer intended to turn down the offer. I spent a feverish night. The next morning proved exasperatingly long. In the afternoon I all but ran to the rendezvous. Yet instead of keeping the appointment I went to lie low in one of my secret hideouts. A lust for that little savage did return to plague me, though I remembered having seen her swim once in an isolated lake, and she had worn an ancient bathing costume far too tight for her, which both clung to and revealed her supple curves. I recalled her rather feline face. Was not her hair redder, her figure fuller than I had cared to remember? Just then, you see, I was imagining her as something approaching a miracle, some sort of vision or almost a playfully diabolic pact: she became both virgin and witch, victim and seductress. And I envisaged her not 'smartly togged out', but wearing that torn bathing costume of indeterminate hue, without which she would turn into a naked woman, just for me. She would show me the russet jungle of her loins, the bush blossoming over that secret at the tops of her thighs. And I was going to be able to inhale her most intimate scents mingled with the aroma of her own sweat. And I could look, look, look.

And do everything, go the whole way.

Make her obey my every whim. I could toy with her flesh, play with her for a mere two hundred sous. Do and see everything. Outstare her green eyes, stick my fingers inside her, think of dirty things to do together.

For two months I hardly dared go out. Her brother never again suggested anything of a similar nature. I was embarrassed whenever I met him . . . In the end, the father went back to prison. The mother left, so they said, to prostitute herself in Orleans. The children followed her or disappeared.

But for a long time to come I reflected on the

look in her green eyes and dwelt upon that indecently tight bathing costume. I should so have liked to collect a pair of short ginger hairs for my private album.

2

I was introduced to Clarisse by my friend André
Jeumont. She was very strictly brought up, the
daughter of an industrialist. Yet she used to go
on holidays alone, to Biarritz, staying with an
aunt who watched over her like a duenna and
who was especially particular about the pedigree
of anyone wanting to keep company with her
niece. In fact Clarisse came from an old, though
petty bourgeois, Basque family. Her sister had
known how to make her mark in Paris – unlike
herself. We would meet Clarisse on the beach,
under the beady eye of her inseparable aunt.

To start with, we only indulged in the sort of
games and remarks children make, for that is
what we still were. Clarisse was very pretty.
Slightly on the chubby side, perhaps, but she
had fine features and her face was gentle and
ingenuous. She always used to wear white
bathing costumes which made her state of semi-
nudity both chaste and exciting. She smiled a
lot and we liked her. As often happened, it was
Jeumont who was most at ease. True, he did

have an athletic build and was goodlooking with it, seeming far older than sixteen. I suspected that Clarisse had a crush on him.

Sometimes there was dancing on the boardwalk at one end of the beach and we would have loved to have gone there with Clarisse. Our main delight was to find a way of distracting the watchdog's attention; in this Clarisse was often the most assiduous, but it was virtually impossible. Another perverse game, invented by Jeumont, consisted of our sitting four or five feet away from the tedious lady, who was usually knitting or reading, and to say reckless or outrageous things just out of earshot. Jeumont, for instance, might remark: 'You must look marvellous under your bathing costume, Clarisse. One of these days we'll take it off you right here, in the middle of the beach.'

Or, 'So today's the day you're going to show us your little pussy, Clarisse. Just you spread your legs a bit while you're sitting on the sand, then pull aside the material between your legs and we'll get a tremendous eyeful.' Clarisse never grew angry, she would simply laugh. That used to upset me and at the same time I would be beside myself, sexually speaking. 'Would you like to feel what I have here below my tummy? Right now it's all hard.' Clarisse would smile and look straight at it: she'd pull a funny face. We were learning scores of dirty words and even dirtier little tricks. Clarisse was none too well-informed but she was a good learner.

One morning Jeumont had to leave for

Switzerland: his father was ill. That was quite all right by me, as it meant I should have Clarisse to myself. I experienced some fleeting anxiety that she might not want me on my own, or that the chaperone might not prove too keen on seeing her exclusively in the company of only one boy. But nothing like that happened. Clarisse remained her usual friendly self. I had trouble continuing André's games, but from the very outset I did start the ball rolling where the one called 'getting rid of the unwanted chaperone' was concerned. On reflection, it seemed to me that Clarisse was quite content to know that the latter was not far away. Clarisse could thus quietly enjoy the expression of our mutual desires without having to worry about their actual fulfilment. Thus she proved more perverse than her face led one to suppose, yet despite everything she continued to be distinctly naive.

It took me a full three days to get round to the dirty talk ritual. On that particular day Clarisse sported a bathing ensemble so well-designed and enticing that although all afternoon its wearer's behaviour was impeccable, I myself burned with ill-suppressed desire. Since I had already glimpsed more than one suggestive hint of her charms, I asked her outright whether she would one day let me see her in the nude.

'You villain! Is that because you love me?'

'I really think I do,' I replied.

She looked at me thoughtfully and what she read in my eyes seemed to astonish her. Everything would have gone on according to the normal routine – she returning to her aunt's, I to my hotel – had it not suddenly begun to rain.

'Quick, back home,' the watchdog aunt called out to us, 'I'll collect our things.'

We did not wait to be asked twice. We ran the whole way back to the villa. Looking over my shoulder, I saw the aunt take shelter under someone's porch, for by now it was pouring.

'Hurry,' said Clarisse.

We dashed up to the first floor and she entered the luxurious lavatory. Without a moment's hesitation she pulled off her costume and sat down on a pouffe in one corner.

'What do you think of me?' she asked, smiling invitingly.

I stood with my back against the door and stared, open-mouthed. She was adorable. Her pose was not vulgar. Indeed, her two pert breasts seemed to peep at me like startled fledglings just visible over the top of their nest. There was a light, tightly curled down on her pubis. I did not manage to see the cleft, which she was concealing between closed thighs.

'You've seen me naked! Go now, my aunt'll be back. I must fetch a bathrobe.'

I left and went downstairs again. The aunt arrived shortly, braving the rain in order not to leave her niece alone one minute longer than absolutely necessary in the company of a young man. A rich young man, it was true, but scarcely a prospect of marriageable age.

'Where is Clarisse?'

'I think she went up to change.'

'Here you are young man,' she said, handing me the shirt and trousers I'd left on the beach and which were fortunately not too wet. 'You go on up and change, too, when she's finished.'

She in fact finished a good half-hour later. I was shivering, but I felt warm enough inside for having seen such a sublime vision and I anticipated delights in store. When I returned to the lavatory and saw that cushion which my darling had so recently favoured with the imprint of her neat little buttocks, I could not help kissing it. This act prompted a massive erection. I had to assuage it, making use of the washbasin, then I ran the taps. Next I dried my whole body vigorously before dressing and rejoining the young girl, her chaperone, and three mugs of steaming chocolate.

Actually nothing further happened for at least a fortnight. I laid siege to Clarisse in vain, making all sorts of advances and believing, like a callow adolescent, that the fact that she had stripped naked for me meant that she was mine for the asking. She did not want to try anything, however, although continuing to give me the gentlest and most encouraging of smiles. She would hold my hand lovingly whenever her aunt was too far off to see us. I tried often enough to convince her that it was possible to escape, to find somewhere more isolated at the far end of the beach, and there in some secluded spot . . . But she would shake her head and invoke her aunt. I used to wonder whether she was scared of finding herself really on her own with me, and was ready to allow certain intimacies behind her aunt's back because she knew that the latter would always rescue her before the point of no return could be reached.

The weather grew so gloomy that we took to playing dominoes. We had more or less had our fill of that when a game of draughts was suggested, for a change. There ensued some discussion about the board and counters which were no longer to be found.

'Perhaps they're in the loft?' the aunt speculated.

'Yes, let's look in the loft. I think there are still some fancy dress outfits and carnival masks up there. We could dress up and play disguises.'

So we climbed up to explore the loft. The aunt stayed behind for a moment or two, searching for candles. When we were up top I felt at ease. As I mentioned earlier, I like the interiors of houses, and their attics always appeal to me most. It was dark up there despite the tiny window and the fanlights. The weather was leaden grey.

'First of all, I'm going to let you see a very sweet little honeybear. I got it when I was about twelve. Give me your hand.'

I gave it her without really thinking. Almost in the same gesture she thrust it under her skirt and wedged it between her ample thighs. I felt the slight rustle of that hairy convexity beneath my palm and fingers, then the sensitive melting flesh. For a second or two I did not react, but I was more relaxed than on the previous occasion and closed my hand, making that furry creature (for it did resemble some tiny animal) adhere to my own skin: I felt it quiver, vibrate momentarily. But the stairs creaked beneath the tread of a panic-stricken mother-hen who had for a few seconds lost sight of her only chick. I promptly let go of the velvet prize. The aunt arrived with a candelabra straight out of some Carpathian castle and we proceeded systematically to search the loft. We disguised ourselves, and in the candlelight the fantasmagoria of our silhouettes – attired as we were in the dress of bygone days – drove us wild with excitement. What was more (and this was for my benefit alone, for my own recurrent fantasies) I knew that neither the little Marquise, the peasant girl, the aristocratic lady, nor the 1789 revolutionary was wearing any knickers. We took turns to disappear behind some hangings and dress up again in some new costume. The duenna seemed vastly entertained. After all, it was within the bounds of credibility that some young relative of hers or a wealthy neighbour had once fucked her in similar circumstances. One never can tell.

My holidays were drawing to an end. André Jeumont had not returned. And I had never again seen Clarisse naked, nor had she ever again offered me that little bearcat of hers to stroke. Sadly I prepared for my departure.

One evening however, in aid of some festival

or other, there were to be fireworks on the beach. We went to them accompanied by our aunt. I call her ours for she had become mine too, by acquisition. On the way back the weather was so pleasantly mild that we stayed outside for a while, chatting about nothing in particular, bodies cool and our hearts all too warm. Yes, life was sweet. Perhaps I was going through a rather melancholy phase. Anyhow, at least everything was going almost for the best, in what was far from the worst of all possible worlds. And already things were not too bad at that.

'Are you leaving early tomorrow?'

'Yes,' I said.

'Do drop by and say goodbye to me. My aunt is off to early Mass and the maid's preparing breakfast then. I'll have a couple of surprises for you.'

She told me this while her aunt had gone to get some refreshments.

The next morning, carrying my suitcase, I rang the front bell. The maid opened the door for me. A table was being laid for breakfast outside, in the sun.

'Mademoiselle will be here soon. She says that the article you've come for, the one you know about, is in the attic.'

I did not understand, but put down my case and climbed up there. It was rather lighter than it had been that first time. I saw Clarisse emerge from behind the hangings; she was in her underwear. Turning round without saying a word, she raised her petticoat. In the half-light her provocative pose, distinctly cruder than the one she had assumed in the lavatory, made my blood race. Her rounded, very feminine buttocks fascinated me and drove me wild: I had an urge to bite them. I knelt down and kissed them impetuously, pressing my tongue into their warm groove, seeking that puckered eyelet concealed at the very core. But she stopped me.

'You must go downstairs again.'

'You're cruel to me,' I said.

She kissed me gently on the lips.

'The second surprise is that you'll see me again in Paris. I'll write or get a message to you.'

I descended and collected my case, greeting the aunt who had just arrived. At a window I saw the lovely Clarisse, clad in a very demure dressing gown, waving to me.

Farewell to the sea and to my love.

3

When I returned home I began my relationship
with Cécile. It turned into something of a
passionate affair, entered into and enjoyed
under the very noses of the family, and at times
seemingly modelled upon children's games;
there were secret dens, hide-and-seek, treasure
hunts too. The house became a labyrinth as it
surrendered its most private corners to us both.
Here we might perhaps just brush lips in
passing, there we could feel one another up
more comprehensively. Every area of the house
took on a new importance, depending upon
what we might require from it. Places which
months earlier left me quite cold now sent me
into ecstasies whenever I dreamed of Cécile. The
coal cellar, which I had known merely as a
name, witnessed our orgasms. The top part of
the gardener's shed would never have tempted
me to any solitary exploration, but one reached
it by ladder; what wonderful, feverish expecta-
tion I endured there when I was first to arrive.
And what an exquisite prologue to our encoun-

ters should Cécile happen to climb up ahead of and above me! There we had discovered sacks, a whole carpet of them, and these we duly soiled, savouring the very distinctive odour which now merged with that strong, clingingly aphrodisiac scent of jute. And there were other elements too, dependent upon sudden spasms of desire, spontaneous moments when we found ourselves unexpectedly alone.

One day my parents decided to have a short holiday on their own. I greatly welcomed that. I could devote myself to Cécile all the more easily. So we came to play at love in those empty rooms belonging to my mother and father. We would meet there secretly – there were always servants around – and carry out a variety of strange rituals in the darkness. We would whisper litanies of obscene then tender words, velvety as our mutual caresses.

Sometimes when the moon was full we could gaze at each other in a tall wardrobe mirror, as we swam in a strange half-light that increased and more than doubled our pleasure. Yet not to be able to see ourselves clearly made us yearn more than ever for that day when we could make love quite naked, in broad daylight, taking our time, all the time we needed to examine our bodies in minutest detail. The sweet scent of her drove me wild and I loved to bury my face in her, devouring the Cécile who smelt of adoles-

cence, of purity itself. Our acts, daring enough
in every sense, were those of gods.

However, one morning when she had not
even finished dressing, I managed to rejoin her
in her room. I found her seated in an armchair
and looking sad and pensive. Her breasts were
free of her unfastened blouse. She was beautiful,
aglow with that rare beauty whose quality is not
and cannot be daily evident. I dearly wished
that that moment could have been prolonged. I
would also have liked her to remain just as she
was on those occasions, inviolate, like some
cherished young animal immune to the process
of ageing. I drew closer to her. She did not turn
her head.

'Cécile,' I said softly.

She still did not look at me. 'What's the
matter?' I asked anxiously. She began to cry. I
was astonished and tried to find out what had
happened. She took a long time to answer and
sobbed in my arms, her whole body shaking. I
felt very moved.

'What is it? Tell me, then.'

I persisted so tenderly that she agreed to do
so.

'Yves, you do realize this can't last, with you
and me. I'm only a servant and you're going to
be very rich. We could never get married.'

I was too embarrassed to reply. Actually – and
this was perhaps egoistic of me, although no
malice or cynical detachment entered into it –
I had given no thought to the future. Totally
involved in my love, caught up in this passion,

I had cocooned myself inside a sort of eternity-in-miniature, without implications for any future, imagining that she too had done likewise. When faced with harsh reality I became distraught. Anyhow, I saw no differences between us, and if I did in that moment understand that obstacles might be placed in our path by my parents and by life itself, I firmly believed that we could cope with them in the course of time. I endeavoured to reassure her.

'No, no, you only think of my body, but you don't love me!'

That seemed absurd to me. And untrue, for I did love her. I was not using her body, I loved it. And despite her initial reticence, I knew all too well how to prove this to her yet again by covering her with caresses since I could not satisfy her with certainties.

But what a lover I had in her! Gentle, tender, warm, thrilling. Eager to fulfil my every desire and to make me sense all of hers. Our relationship took on a strange new lease of life. She would, for instance, often change her hairstyle, and this usually made her seem older or it coarsened her features.

Then, on another miraculous day, we found overselves alone again – Cécile examining herself in a bedroom mirror in the villa we had at Dinard. My parents had gone on an excursion to Mont-Saint-Michel, I had invented a visit to a friend, Cécile pleaded a headache. The servants were on vacation or had gone to the beach.

This time she had altered her hairstyle

completely. It made her look like a goddess from the classical era, the age of absolute beauty. And I was to discover this vision, revealed for my own delectation and mine alone, in that baroque villa beside the sea. I had saved my pocket money in order to buy her an expensive necklace. She tried it on, nude as she was. She let it hang right down to the subtle fleece below her stomach, to that proof of adult self-assurance. I tried to nibble at that entire fringe festival, her hirsute carnival of moist flesh mingled with costly pearls. Then I tasted the delicate liquid welling between her thighs, trickling like a fresh rivulet through moss. And in the mirror I transfixed her with a shaft as hard as one of Cupid's own arrows while for the first time she turned her back to me, upon me. Then, also for the first time in my life, I penetrated my love via the tempting tightfurled ring, thus espousing the devil. True, this fundamentally lecherous act was hotly and mutually desired, a sort of diabolic union and communion. She had knowingly led me on when, adopting a shamelessly sluttish posture, she had leaned over with her back towards the mirror, ostensibly to be able to see herself, to stare through and between her legs and to inspect her most private parts, spreading wide the cheeks of her arse. This supreme vision caused me to plummet into the abyss. Yet she'd merely been admiring herself somewhat ingenuously, declaring that she had 'rather a nice figure' with 'hidden charms, at that'.

Ah, Cécile, I love you still!

* * *

When my parents were at home we would have to keep our wits about us, inventing special signals, finding and making excuses. Misers of our secret, deceptive pleasures, we hoarded every minute. We were cheating on society, having to thieve our sublimer moments. Should one of us climb up to the attic, the other would soon find a pretext for looking for some item in his or her room. This would all take place pretty briskly. One would then swiftly go upstairs where the other was keeping a look-out and would open the door. There, always in the murk, our lips would almost bruise in their frenzy as our hands groped greedily over our bodies. My hand used to bury itself between her thighs, finding that soft furrow as if it were an endlessly new discovery. In turn her hand, as though by chance, closed round my urgent desire, which invariably surprised by its inexorable rigidity and sheer 'presence'; indeed, for her this wilful actor always did play an imposing, impressive part.

Yet once we had left Dinard behind, our love too had to adapt to winter. Sometimes there was occasion to search for wood in the shed at the bottom of the garden. She liked being on duty and sensing that I was outside on the prowl. When I saw her outlined in the open doorway, I used to run and hide in that shed. She would arrive, enter and know by intuition that I was there in the shadow. Furiously, gropingly we would embrace. Breathing grew noisier, faster: we outdid each other in our febrile haste. Then, offering herself, she would lie down, legs apart. She often dispensed with underwear, or she would wear a variety of split knickers still fashionable in those days, and these she would swiftly shed. I used to go crazy feeling her abandoned wriggles and desperate pressures against me: I'd even have unbuttoned beforehand, in readiness. And there in the friendly pitch dark, redolent of the wholesome scent of wood, there at the far end of the garden yet so near others, we stole our keen and hurried pleasure. Sometimes we would only fondle our sexes. On other occasions, with increasing deftness, I would simply manipulate her. Our orgasms were always rapidly induced and we would gasp out all kinds of silly remarks.

I had once seen the dark-eyed, intense Cécile, clad only in a plain shift and shoes and stockings, sprawled feline and languid across an ornate armchair. She brought to mind that celebrated image which represents the Muse of Automatic Writing so dear to the Surrealists. That day I saw her as the goddess of a particular kind of lust. The one only its initiates can savour. The muse of the mental picture, of cerebral scoptophilia. For me, the Muse of Happiness. On the following day, after working on it all night, I read her a prose-poem which (I most modestly confess) had considerable style. It was demented, possibly ill-written, but it definitely did have something. As she was intelligent, she knew I was pleased with it.

One Sunday morning when her aunt was absent, Cécile was working in the kitchen. I arrived and she locked the door. Despite the open window, and although anyone might have passed or been surprised to find the door locked, she unbuttoned me briskly and knelt down. She bent over my prick which she had released from its customary abode and which she then proceeded to suck and lick until it unloaded its agitated freight upon the tiled floor of the kitchen. Cécile dried me off thereafter with tiny towellings of the tongue.

On another occasion there was a power-cut. I happened to be close to Cécile and dragged her into a corner. And there, while everyone else bustled past us looking for candles, I hoisted up her skirts, ripped down her knickers and, with my own wicked wick undipped, for the space of several heady seconds let my avid mouth avail itself of a moistly aromatic essence.

The following May, Cécile was pregnant. She did not want to name me as the father, whereas I kept telling her we could get married. She went back home to her native Aquitaine without even letting me know – I was at school at the time. I ran away, trying to rejoin her. When I arrived at her home, they told me she had gone to stay with her grandmother. I returned home. Later I received a letter to the effect that she had given birth to a boy whom she had called Yves. She had found a good job with a local solicitor. A short while afterwards I learned that she had married this solicitor, a bachelor in his forties. I was happy to know that her future looked rosy. But I suffered overwhelming sadness. Why had she fled from me? I thought of her once again, and of the way she had stood in front of the mirror, so beautiful with her pearl necklace, her splendid breasts and her voluptuous, entrancing young body. So ready to give herself to me. So ready to lose herself in ecstasy.

Cécile . . . My Cécile!

4

Tired of Paris and of acquaintances that had become too predictable and familiar, I left in search of solitude. I wandered around Provence like a typical intellectual, supposedly working out my youthful distaste for people in general. Provence was considerable consolation, with its unspoilt villages and those parched towns patched with shade from their lime-trees, and where the maze of winding alleys would suddenly open out onto spacious squares , mistily moist in the cool spray of the fountains. I would also glance casually at girls, although I kept up the pose of not even being aware of them. They were playful brunettes mainly, who seemed to crack my sidelong looks between their white teeth or drown them in their dark brown eyes. The speech of these girls had a sun-ripened lilting accent and they responded to glances of admiration, however sly, with garlands of delightful smiles.

* * *

I had stopped the car in a small market town. Suddenly I spotted her the other side of the square, at the entrance to an alleyway. Against a mischievous sun, her body was clearly outlined in its virtually transparent white dress. She was evidently much taken with a very fine and glossy black tomcat which, exuding due feline pride, was allowing himself to be stroked. She rewarded the animal by murmuring endearments and making a great fuss of him. He seemed to enjoy that. Even from a distance, I myself found the tableau quite exquisite. But the nearer I drew, the more I was convinced I recognized her. Who was she? Then I had a sudden brainwave, the very moment she chose to look at me.

'Yves!' she exclaimed.

Her memory was keener than mine, or maybe I had changed less than she had.

'Anne!'

How vivacious and attractive she was, dressed like a holidaymaker! And what a friendly smile.

'What became of your pigtails?'

'They bit the dust, along with my milk-teeth.'

'Liar, you never had any milk-teeth, you just had big fangs with little gaps. All the better to bite me with.'

She laughed loudly at that, obviously happy to see me. As for myself, I was overjoyed. Quite by chance I had met that little girl again – the one I remembered as rather skinny, yet pretty with her light brown pigtails – and here she was transformed into a beautiful young woman. If she seemed like a stranger, or her new appearance at least was disconcerting, I now had the opportunity of getting to know her. And to know her very well indeed.

'How long has it been?' I asked.

'Five years.'

'Too long, far too long.'

For the rest of that day we were inseparable. What was she doing there? Well, she was lodging for a week with the grandmother of an employee of her parents. I accordingly decided to find myself an hotel.

Every morning we went for a swim in a small lake outside the town. In the afternoons we would lounge around in deckchairs or go for a stroll or a car trip. One day we ventured almost as far as the coast. That evening I kissed her for the first time (as an adult), beneath a canopy of stars and to an intoxicating obbligato of cicadas. The night was warm. Living and loving were sweet.

She invited me to spend a few days with her at her home in the Auvergne. Only the servants were there. We were still playing like children, going shrimping and mushroom-picking. In the evenings we used to have long philosophical discussions or we would talk about books and literary articles we had read and liked. She was always rather vague and casual, and when she sat curled up or cross-legged on an armchair I invariably got a good view of firm, slender thighs and what was between them: although fine lace covered most of the prominent curve of her mount, a black astrakhan frill peeped from either edge, a stark contrast with the white material. For several days I ascribed her careless-ness to innocence. Yet I noticed a more artful pose, a knowing look, and these convinced me that there was an element of covert invitation.

One evening when she had once again proffered me the usual generous view, I knelt down and placed my lips against her inner thigh – that thigh I recalled as being skinny, wiry, child-like. She shuddered, but when my fingers reached the lace fringe as if to pull it aside, she sat forward.

'No Yves, you mustn't,' she said in a dull tone.

I was rather annoyed, and getting to my feet again, replied eventually: 'And why not?'

'Because . . .'

She seemed equally annoyed at having to give a reason.

'Well, because we're not . . . married . . . nor engaged.'

'What a good little bourgeoise you are.'

I was angry and I went to bed. After a while I grew thirsty – for I had been reading rather than sleeping – and I went downstairs again. She was still in the drawing-room, sitting in the same chair. I went over to her, thinking she had fallen asleep there. I noticed she was wide awake, however, and I was worried by her rather gaunt, hollow-eyed expression: she must have been crying. I leaned across and kissed her on the forehead very tenderly.

'Anne,' I said, 'I love you.'

She did not react to this immediately and I grew anxious. At last she said: 'Is it true? Is that really true?'

'I love you. I always have.'

And I was not lying. There had been Clarisse, certainly. (But that had been mere childishness, albeit somewhat depraved.) And there had been Cécile, but by then I could admit to myself that that consuming and immoderate passion was in every respect doomed to failure. As for my sweet pigtailed one, I loved her not so much carnally or cerebrally than in another, deeper sense. I loved her for an infinity of memories we had in common, for secrets shared, and because together we had discovered the green Eden of youthful affection. It went without saying: I loved her as one loves an article of faith, balm to soothe the conscience.

'I love you,' I repeated.

We remained sitting with our arms around each other, not talking much. Dawn took us by surprise. And in that rosy pallor we walked along a dewy path which led down to a small pool. There we swam through early mist, amid a loudening chorus of birdsong. Our love was even lovelier than a lake.

But our relationship continued to be platonic. During our evenings Anne would occasionally resume her favourite pose, the one revealing her upper thighs and groin. One night after dining in a small restaurant where we had drunk rather too much wine and liqueurs, we were chatting drowsily in front of the dying fire. She assumed her customary posture. I laid my cheek against the underside of one thigh and she said nothing. My lips softly brushed her lovenest through the material. As though in a dream I heard her say: 'Lick me through the material, if you like.'

I complied, trying to capture a fragrance through the silken screen, to sink into contours that led ever deeper. Soon the fine material was sopping and sticky. I continued, plunging ever deeper, working with great sweeps of the tongue and sometimes entrapping her precious pubis wholly within my mouth. She was moaning. I did not want to draw aside the wet silk. To me at the time this mode of 'respecting' her seemed madly perverted.

For nearly an entire week we never went further than that. Her parents returned, but I was prevailed upon to stay.

I received a letter one morning, which surprised me since I had told nobody where I was. Opening it, I found it was only a few lines long and the handwriting was obviously disguised. *Monsieur* (it read), *if you want to find out something to your advantage, which you don't yet know about Anne d'Evremont, be at Queue-de-l'Etang Farm, Thursday 5 p.m. A friend and well-wisher.*

Conflicting emotions beset me and my head

began to spin. I trusted Anne and would have liked to let her in on this message, but conversely it might worry her also, the next day being Thursday. I wanted to find out the identity of this friend who wished me so well and punch him on the nose.

That Thursday I was on the point of not going to the farm in question. But it just so happened that Anne had gone into town to see the local dressmaker. I therefore decided to go there without more ado and settle accounts with my benevolent friend. It was raining slightly and I ran most of the way. The farm was silent and open for the very good reason that it had long since been abandoned. Outside the front door the grass had grown thick and tall. I felt rather uneasy and was on my guard, expecting some trap. At last I knocked lightly on the door. The sound echoed inside but brought no response. I turned the handle and pushed. The door opened.

To my amazement the interior was perfectly maintained. A piece of paper on the kitchen table caught my eye. It read, again in big capital letters: *Monsieur Morhant, meet me in the end room.* My friend might not amount to much, but he did not lack a certain sense of the conspiratorial. I went through to the end room. The room was darkened and at first I could distinguish nothing, then I made out a figure lying on the bed.

'Open the shutters a little,' a voice commanded.

I did so and when I turned the vision I saw was a dazzling one. She lay face down and full-length across the bed, not quite naked, but in her underwear, waiting. The drawstrings of her satin culottes were untied and there before me were the finest pair of buttocks – their curves of a positively lunar amplitude – which I had ever contemplated. She was flaunting herself, stretched out there in her flimsy finery of satin and lace, like a Christmas present, an open casket. It was indeed the best gift imaginable, the most desirable reward for my restraint. Yet this very feminine rump, so provocatively and tastefully displayed, dispelled all my previous assumptions, since deep down I suppose I still thought of Anne as a little girl. But here she was – a woman – and a ripely sexual woman too. I drew closer, my throat dry. She was looking at me over one rounded shoulder, a youthful breast now visible.

I paid eager homage to her posterior opulence, hugging and squeezing her haunches and kissing them with delight and enthusiasm. By baring them fully I was able to admire that whole soft femininity, an area of velvet valleys, of pink and white splendours. I revelled in it, sharing her ardour and melting in that welcome, and soon that intimate symphony of groans and sighs welled over us both, while I stroked, massaged, palped and finally penetrated. Then I was free to initiate a rhythm that led us to ecstasy, making her gasp and wheeze in her joyous paroxysms. And we whispered too, our words soft and tender, then urgently stammered and turning finally into a full scale crescendo of erotic delirium.

She informed me later that her parents had recently purchased the farm, intending it to be a sort of haven for guests of theirs who loved the countryside. As for us, we loved only the darkened interiors of rooms whose mattresses were firm and resilient in the cool shadow. Almost every day we would devote a couple of hours or so to a journey back in time, recreating that closed and bygone world of the great libertines, the classical age of erotica, mad Marquises and all.

It was one of the ironies of fate that I received a second anonymous letter written in much the same style and informing me unequivocally that Anne was very far from being chaste, and that she had had 'scores of lovers and affairs'. I did not choose to believe it. But the seeds of doubt were sown. Everything that might confirm the note's assertions, each possible lie that led to any corroboration however slight, all combined to make me more suspicious, more embittered.

Our love ended with the summer. And with it our friendship.

5

I am speaking of my first love affairs, my first true loves, in chronological order. Yet Céline is harder to place, for though she definitely succeeded Clarisse and Cécile, I cannot be quite sure that she did not precede Anne. More confusingly, hers too was a reappearance in my life. At the start, this was a romance conducted through an intermediary. So it was odd, and strangely exciting too.

Cécile had left me in the May of my seventeenth year. At the end of that summer, the beginning of the autumn term, I joined the lower sixth form. On All Saints' Day or thereabouts I was taking a thoroughly romantic, self-absorbed stroll, when along one park avenue I happened to meet three rather vivacious girls, who were nonetheless well-behaved and ignored me completely. All three were attractive, but one in particular appealed to me. Every male has his own idea of what a young girl should be like.

She was my ideal precisely: the perfect image, in that rare state of grace which lasts only two or three years, something resembling the aura of a pubescent girl, or the maturer woman's post-coital glow.

She had a pink flush about her complexion, and I imagined her suffused with a halo of eternal youth. I did not admire her by way of any notion of virginity, but more for the impression she gave of being beyond reach of all impurity, light years away from evil. Despite that, I continued to fantasise about her body: I saw it as creamy-white and a dreamlike pink; that body had to be neat, clean, sweet-smelling, a vision of rose and alabaster. Although I had had some sexual experience by then, such a creation did not seem misplaced, for perhaps I needed purity.

I saw her again several times before Christmas, either on her own or with friends. I knew she went to the local girls' school.

It happened just after the New Year. I was with another newly-promoted sixth former at the time, a youth I thought vulgar but who had pursued me and virtually pressganged me into a form of friendship with him. On the pavement opposite we saw a group of girls gossiping about their various student misadventures. One young girl, 'my' girl, was listening, smiling slightly, but her smile seemed to me merely polite and sociable; more that of an outsider, in fact. I was pleased by her demeanour. My newfound 'friend' had noticed my interest.

'Do you think that girl's nice-looking?' he inquired.

I looked at him, somewhat appalled.

'I think she's beautiful,' I replied curtly.

He sniggered, retorting: 'Don't get worked up, old man. But if you like I can tell you quite a few things about that girl.'

With this he gave a little nod in her direction as if to make it absolutely clear to whom he referred. His comments, along with the gesture, made my heart sink.

'I know her very well. Very well indeed.'

The revolting creature was taking his revenge.

'People always say that. To hear most of them talk you'd think every single one of them had slept with every girl in town, married women included.'

'Look, dear boy, I promise you I'm telling the truth: I've slept with her and I've seen her in the buff too, masses of times.'

I could gladly have hit him. As for that expression 'in the buff', first it annoyed, then destroyed me: my young girl would never be 'in the buff'. Nude, yes, but 'in the buff', no.

'Right, goodbye then,' I said, eager to escape from him.

'As you like. But she's my sister.'

A number of thoughts rushed through my head: could she really be the sister of such a common and unintelligent boy? Might she be incestuous? Was he taking me for a ride?

He was amused by my all too evident surprise, then he became friendly again.

'I slept in the same bed as her, three or four times. That was about twelve years ago . . .'

'Was it then that you saw her with no clothes on?'

'Yes. But I've seen her starkers since.'

'You're lying.'

'You think she's embarrassed, eh? I know damn well what she looks like, old man.'

That day I preferred to change the subject. But it gnawed at me. And a week later, after I'd caught sight of the young girl again, I went up to Edgar in the schoolyard and engaged him in conversation, hoping to get on to the topic of his sister. He seemed astonished that it was I who had accosted him. Yet he had the good grace to converse with me, and I, of course, returned to my favourite obsession. He made some surprising revelations which did not quite tally with the image I had built up of his sister, but these I was easily able to incorporate later to her own, and my fantasy's, advantage. Although her behaviour in public was reserved, at home she liked to display herself naked. She enjoyed walking around in the nude and coming out of the bathroom with nothing on. She was quite shameless in a 'family' context. Besides there was nothing in a nice figure to be ashamed of, especially if one was in one's own home. What unwholesome desires could there be within one's own family?

On the subject of unwholesome desires, I suspected her brother nurtured a few, although he told me that nothing incestuous had ever

66

taken place between them. He had, however, a peculiar way of relating his sister's 'adventures', a barely repressed enjoyment. And he was also the possessor of a sadistic streak: he would draw my attention to a particularly suggestive detail, for instance, or he might deliberately delay telling me something he maintained was highly significant. He told me his sister's name only after a whole fortnight had elapsed. The name promptly became part of me, I found myself writing it down and underlining it on every conceivable occasion when there was paper to hand. And I would repeat it incessantly whenever I lay on that boarding-school bed and let lovingly imagined pictures float before me, images which Edgar had cunningly sneaked into my consciousness. I used to think that he was exaggerating. What was more, I hated him for two basic reasons: he could see Céline at will in intimate circumstances, and he discussed her in a way I thought objectionable.

He had also admitted to me that on various occasions their father, whose hobby was painting, had been happy to have his daughter pose in the nude for him. Edgar described her pose: 'Standing quite naked, one knee resting on the cushion of an armchair. It was a portrait of her viewed from the back. Her head was turned, looking over her shoulder, and her face had a madonna's expression but the whole position made her bum stick out.' The vulgar phrase jarred on me, yet I was craven enough to let it pass because he was useful to me: I did not want to lose contact with Céline.

He never failed to undermine my infatuation. Came the day I asked him to take a note to his sister, and he agreed to do so. When I saw him again the day after, I was anxious, restless, feverishly impatient. He decided for three whole break-periods to discuss nothing but the weather and other banalities. That evening I managed to catch him on his way home and, swallowing my pride, asked him if he had delivered my note.

'Yes and we both had a good laugh. She even read it out to the family over dinner.'

Then he sauntered off, braying like a donkey. What shame, what treachery! Yet had he told me the truth? From other sources I had discovered that Céline's family consisted of eccentrics who scarcely even spoke to their neighbours and kept very much to themselves, living in a vast mansion surrounded by an extensive garden. No one really knew what went on in that household.

The end of the academic year came round. I could not continue to keep in touch with Céline, nor bring myself to confront her. I changed schools, coming to Paris. Three years later, after numerous misadventures, I was to meet Anne, with the results I have described.

It was autumn, after that idyll in the Auvergne, when I made the discovery. Wandering down the Rue de Seine, nose pressed to the windows of the art shops and galleries for which the street is celebrated, I saw in one small dark gallery a painting which greatly attracted me. It was a nude, rendered with photographic precision. I walked in. The old fellow who had the task of selling the various fashionably daring or pretentious pictures stocked there charged towards me, while I myself made a beeline for the portrait. I had another shock then: I knew the sitter. Or else the model uncannily resembled her, for it certainly did look like Céline.

'She's beautiful, no doubt about that,' remarked the diminutive procurer of rude nudes.

'Who's the artist?'

'Jean Modot.'

The name meant nothing to me. Her father immediately sprang to my mind, but perhaps it was a pseudonym or by another painter altogether. I asked the price, and he named a disastrous sum (as far as my own student funds were concerned), claiming that the artist was highly rated. I paid him a sizeable deposit, requesting him to reserve it for me. Then I asked him for the artist's address, which he gave me without quibbling.

The artist was indeed called Jean Modot. He was aged about forty and his studio was in Montparnasse. It was excellently-lit and enormous, so I guessed he was well off. There were only two nudes, which were obviously of professional models. The other paintings were portraits (either head and shoulders or full-scale) of rich people, mostly women, and mostly exuding superiority and vacuous self-importance, although some were pleasant enough.

'I paint only a very few nudes,' he told me. 'My clientele is rather bourgeois, apart from some minor aristocracy. Occasionally, for my own relaxation, I do hire a model and paint her either partly clothed or nude.'

He confirmed he had painted the picture I'd purchased at the little gallery.

'That's not my usual gallery. There's a rather special story behind that painting.'

I urged him to tell it me but he refused. I therefore admitted that I knew the young girl he had painted and that I had been in love with her. He smiled at that, but somewhat ruefully.

'I was in the same boat as yourself my dear sir, and so I shall let you in on the real story.'

Céline, for it was indeed Céline, had turned up at Modot's one day and begged him to paint her portrait. Then she specified that he paint her in the nude. He refused, making it clear that nudes were not his particular speciality.

'Well, be like Goya and the Maja, paint just my face, sketch out a full-length reclining pose, and get a model for the body.'

He agreed. Meanwhile he fell in love with Céline. She always resisted his advances, however. And she never came back to collect her portrait. By way of revenge, he had taken it to that little merchant of nudes for the bedroom

– and doubtless by appointment purveyor to the provincial brothels.

I never went back to Modot's. But I had managed to obtain Céline's address. One day I lay in wait outside and intercepted her as she was leaving her flat.

'Céline!'

She turned and seemed to recognize me. Then she greeted me with a smile.

'Well sir,' she said, 'you're rather fickle. I received one love letter from you, via my brother, but he never brought me another.'

I reminded her of how she had behaved.

'My brother lied. Come for a walk with me in the Luxembourg Gardens.'

And what I had so often romantically dreamed, so often yearned to experience, came about in the simplest manner imaginable. That very evening Céline was mine.

Despite the shady aspects of Céline's life and despite what her brother had told me about her, I fell madly in love with her.

Yes, I could still recall Edgar describing Céline's fascination when watching two dogs fuck, and how by his account she had stayed observing them to the very end. Céline posing nude for her father. Céline living in a house that certain of my schoolfriends considered little better than a bordello. Céline painted, perhaps in the nude, by a Jean Modot who – in spite of what he had told me – had also been profoundly aroused by her.

Did she conform to the generally accepted view of a young girl, or was she more like the muse demystified by Baudelaire in one of his aphorisms?

Yet that image I first formed of her was not quick to disappear. And even though I understood she was no virgin when she gave herself to me, she still remained, for me, an icon of purity, and my projection of that quality.

When, that day in her apartment (where she lived alone) she welcomed me, undressing, lying open for me, exposing her twinned firm little buttocks, their pert curves so sublimely rounded, and when my questing tongue led me to the revelation that she too had a moisture, a scent of desire – even then that image of her was by no means blurred.

Which is why I (perhaps) married Céline and (perhaps) had a child by her.

6

For a long time my history teacher was Mme
Morin. Her face was not particularly attractive
and it showed the wear and tear of her forty
years. I suspected, however, that her body was
a different matter. On the whole, though, her
cool and daunting appearance did not stir us to
any sexual thoughts. At that time André
Jeumont was my classmate. He was the son of
a wealthy banker.

Although our parents were rich, this haughty
lady, who could frequently be sour-tempered
and caustic, used to pick on us both. That year
we had a new Biology teacher. She was a pretty
little woman, if rather dreary, and she soon
became friendly with Mme Morin. One day the
latter made a very offensive comment about
André, and from that moment on André's
hatred of 'la Morin' knew no bounds.

After the Easter holidays, and during the
summer term, André, who had just got back
from a stay in Switzerland, came up to me all
smiles.

'Something's up!' he said mysteriously. 'Will you go along with me or not?'

'In what?'

'First just tell me if you trust me, that's all.'

'Yes,' I said, intrigued.

He was content with that. During recreation I spotted him looking towards a corner of the courtyard, giggling away to himself. Following his stare I saw Mme Morin chatting to the young Biology teacher. André's expression was one of malicious delight.

'You've still got it in for her, haven't you?' I said as I went up to him.

'And how. Do you know what those two are?'

'Teachers,' I blithely replied.

'Ah yes, well, perhaps . . . But they teach something else too. Because first and foremost those two are dykes.'

I stared at him in amazement.

'And I'm going to get my revenge!'

The plan was simple. Mme Morin was the widow of a young teacher killed in 1916. She lived alone and had a small flat in that same town where we were at school. Jeumont was from Paris, but he had spent a lot of his free time spying on Mme Morin. It seemed that the younger teacher often went round to her place. Anyhow, after her first term at the school she had given up her hotel room and had gone to lodge with Mme Morin. Perhaps there was nothing suspicious in that, but one night

Jeumont climbed over the wall, reached her flat and with considerable daring managed to see enough to confirm his theory of a lesbian relationship.

While in Switzerland he worked on the idea of revenge. His family owned a vast property which included a small hunting-lodge. He had spent part of his vacation preparing it. The lodge-keeper was a dignified old man who knew the history of the region backwards. By then Jeumont had also discovered something else about Mme Morin: ever since her honeymoon she had been a devotee of that whole Alpine region, even going so far as to write an *Informal History of French-Speaking Switzerland*. Everything fell into place. The lodge-keeper's complicity had to be ensured: it was necessary to persuade him that the entire scheme was just a harmless student prank. Jeumont worked hard on this, wheedling and cajoling him. The old man was happy to go along. The idea of playing host to two relatively young women, teachers what was more, and of proving to them that the role of elderly expert which he was being asked to play was in fact justified – all this certainly flattered his self-esteem, if not his vanity into the bargain.

He was therefore assigned to write the lady an appreciative letter praising her book and inviting her and any friend of her choice to spend a few days on 'his estate'. We made certain this offer would be timed to suggest the Whitsun holiday period, when for all our parents knew we ourselves would be off camping. We heard that

75

the Morin woman had accepted the invitation and intended bringing a friend. Our plan was working.

André had taken great pains with the hunting-lodge bedroom where our two teachers were to sleep. It looked impressive with its vast hangings, fur rugs and canopies – a real love-nest in fact, but one which contained two hidden cameras.

On the very first evening we soon realised the ladies were 'at it'. When before us we saw Mme Morin's bottom bared by her friend's assiduous attentions, we turned pale, then we found ourselves blushing. It was truly quite a shock to see the actual private parts of a teacher exposed, especially when the adult in question appeared to consider us as members of a lesser and stupid species. This was revenge indeed. She was a woman just like any other, one with buttocks, hair between her thighs and a carnivorous flower with aromatic juices. The lining of that curtain probably bears the traces of our extreme excitement to this very day. The delicate fingers of those ladies sank into their fleecy mounts, dug inside their soft cracks, probed even into the Socratic eyelet. We knew their favourite underwear, their terms of endearment, all their perverted activities. What a treat! It was alarming. At no time however did we show ourselves, but André did succeed in taking some good, i.e. compromising, photographs. There was one in particular, taken when they had only just returned from a walk, which showed Morin spanking the younger teacher's bottom with a shoe – on a mere pretext, at that, since Mme Morin was often given to exert her authority.

Later I realised why Jeumont was not keen to show himself. Firstly, so as not to alert the old keeper, his parents or the women, and secondly because the situation might misfire: they could accuse us of having lured them into a trap, forced them to undress and so on. He had, finally, an even subtler and deadlier vengeance in mind.

On almost the first day back from the holiday, he asked me to stay on with him after one of the Morin woman's classes.

He went up to her desk and respectfully asked permission to show her a document of the utmost interest on the subject of Switzerland. She consented, both pleased and curious. From a big envelope he pulled out the photograph in which the young biology teacher lay on top of her, simultaneously introducing one slim finger into a very personal orifice. At the sight of naked flesh, she was ready to wax indignant, when she suddenly if not quite immediately recognised herself. Whereupon she turned pale, flushed and became utterly speechless.

'In one day, every pupil and teacher in this school, along with the Headmaster, the Regional Schools Inspector and even the Minister of Education, could be sent this photograph . . .

not to mention a few other ones. The game's up. So now lift your skirt and let's have a feel!'

The tone of voice – André addressing her with the informal 'tu' – stunned her like a slap in the face. She therefore took some time to comply. With a glance she made sure the door was properly closed, then, taking cover behind her rostrum chair, she meekly pulled up her dress to reveal a gorgeous pair of knickers. Jeumont demanded she remove them. Nervous and flushed, she did so. The action – almost obscene in that place consecrated to study, that temple of learning whose high priestess she had been – sent us into transports of excitement. Jeumont grabbed the knickers (which he kept) and sniffed them disgustedly. Then he made Mme Morin bend over the bench that he and I usually shared and there he went at her from the rear. I kept watch by the door, but that in no way allayed her fear of being discovered in her unequivocal posture. On the other hand, her panic merely increased André's ardour and he showed her no mercy. I could hear the damp slap of flesh against flesh, the squeak of table-legs, and Jeumont's occasional crude comments. We then changed places and it was my turn to bury myself deep in Mme Morin, who was by now dripping wet.

The teacher ended her day bare-bottomed beneath her dress, and this fact greatly excited us the more we dwelt upon it. She was available to us.

After we had gone off for a good laugh, our

attentions and desires over the next few days turned towards the young Biology teacher. As for Morin, she was obliged to submit to our little whims until the end of the school year.

She got herself transferred to darkest Africa.

7

My brief romance with the cinema was precocious but profitable. First, an anecdote. I had
been much impressed by the 'bathing beauties'
of that period. And their voluptuous if
mannered charms often used to feature in my
erotic dreams.

For me the perfect 'bathing beauty' was the
mother of my pigtailed friend. I don't know
why. Or rather I do: I had seen her in her
bathing costume beside a lake in the Auvergne.
After our encounter in the attic, I was invited to
stay at her house. I accepted mainly because
of those pigtails I so cherished. Very early one
morning we had secretly arranged to go
shrimping. I had already gone downstairs on
the sly to make us a coffee and some sand-
wiches. The expedition with all its secrecy was
now to take on a rather different dimension of
adventure.

I was just about to go and wake my girlfriend
when, coming out of the kitchen, I ran into Mme
d'Evremont sitting at the foot of her staircase.

She was scantily clad to say the least, and she sat there lacing up her very stylish boots. A cheeky peaked cap perched jauntily on her head and made her look more than ever like some denizen of Hollywood. I took one step too many and she caught sight of me.

'Ah Yves, it's you,' she said, not at all startled. 'I'm getting ready to go snailing. Are you coming?'

'It's funny weather to go hunting snails. Or rather, it's a funny outfit of yours.'

She laughed. 'I like to feel comfortable. And perhaps I might meet some romantic man . . .'

At that I drew closer to her and gave way to what I had so far refused myself. I dropped down beside her, level with her knees, and parted those generous thighs of hers. I exposed a sparsely-thatched but throbbing sex that looked wondrously, cavernously deep. An audacious Ali Baba, I used my tongue and lips to Open Sesame, then my shaking hands roved over her soft, opulent quivering flesh and squeezed her plump buttocks. She turned round and then, almost on my knees also and clumsily ensconced, I possessed her frenziedly as animals do, intoxicated by her hot wet grotto, my belly slapping loud against her white flanks. She too was moaning like a wild thing.

I could never be sure whether or not her eldest daughter Nadine had seen us, that day.

It was Henri de Chareyre, a confirmed lecher,

who introduced me to Helga Jungblut, better known as Helena Junebelle. This well-upholstered actress was in all respects utterly pretentious. Every conceivable vice was attributed to her and I think she even went so far as to invent yet more for herself. But I was fascinated by the vast white arse she used to display to us, invariably wobbling over black stockings.

She would adopt very cinematic poses (in the costume biography genre), and indulge in obscene dances in order to arouse Henri and myself to a state of erotic excitement. Our blonde German had once appeared in a film called *The Hotel Broad*, playing the part of a thief who falls in love with a Prince. She repeated this role for us in private and more sexily. She became a broad enough broad (especially in the beam) and one who showed no reluctance about showing her pussy either.

She awoke our instincts towards flagellation and sodomy. We did not even need to ask, but simply let her have it on her enticing hindquarters, either via a succession of resounding spankings that rained down on those creamy flanks or through penetrations not in the rulebook and which were always accompanied by mildly sadistic wrestling-matches with the fleshy globes we squeezed black and blue.

One evening she made a bet with us: she intended to go and lie down on a beach wearing something nearer to a fishing net than a good old *cache-sexe*. We certainly could not have restrained her, had we known how, and she won her bet. She scored a considerable success with the assorted young folk who frequented that beach, also with some elderly gentlemen, war veteran types in the habit of going out for a breath of fresh air, sporting their decorations and all. I suspect she recruited a few more lovers here and there. The younger set could safely graze upon her superb bosom but only as long as it took for her to seduce the innocent; she allowed the older ones to prostrate themselves in worship under her Junoesque posteriors. And I could not help forming mental pictures of their dignified, hoary heads being all but crushed beneath those arrogant cruppers. Nor could I stop smiling. Nor stop myself coming.

I could reconstruct this scene photographically only by using my favourite mare, my special hostess, and she lent herself to it with enthusiasm. As I too had aged somewhat, I could savour having my head sat upon by a generous rump.

During the period of my life when I was dabbling at painting, I had an extraordinary adventure. It was winter and I was strolling along a canal, probably the Orleans one. Too much the dreamer to be thinking about sketching, I was admiring the various tones of pink, white, grey and pale blue. Suddenly I caught sight of a barge. A handful of snow was sifting down upon it. What was it doing there? It was the only barge moored in this spot, so far from any hamlet or village. I had just produced my sketchbook when the cabin door opened. A woman emerged. Even from quite far away I knew it was a woman, for she was stark naked. She did not see me to start with, but was pre-occupied in doing something I couldn't distin-guish. When she did see me, she disappeared immediately.

I approached, intrigued. A man now came out, but he was fully dressed.

'You have just chanced upon a little interlude, Monsieur,' he said with a slight accent I couldn't place, 'which you could not have anticipated on such a cold day.'

'And very delightful too.'

'You seem to be taking notes. I hope I'm not being inquisitive?'

'No, not at all. Please excuse me, I was making a sketch of your boat and the countryside.'

'Are you a painter?'

'Strictly Sundays.'

The man saw the joke and began laughing.

'Please come aboard.'

His name was Hans von Ackenau. He was German by extraction, Count by inheritance and photographer by choice. He invited me to look around. Various photographic apparata had been installed in the cabin. The Count raised a heavy curtain and I then had my first big surprise. It looked like the interior of a Symbolist harem or a high-priced brothel.

Half-naked women, several more completely nude, were lounging or sprawling on cushions, bearskins and a variety of rare or valuable animal hides and furs. The sides of the cabin were adorned with Oriental carpets, and a large stove threw out a veritable furnace heat. I couldn't even bring myself to count the women at first. Finally I did work out that there were nine in all. The oldest was no more than thirty, while at least two of them were scarcely sixteen.

'I appreciate your astonishment, but I'm very well off. Besides, this barge was already fitted up when I bought it. It's never – or anyway not for a very long time – served to carry freight. It's a floating brothel, good and improper.'

I still did not dare scrutinize the young women, although they themselves looked me over in leisurely fashion. They responded to my air of embarrassment by giggling shamelessly. The Count noticed.

'Mesdemoiselles, Monsieur is my guest. I consider that to make fun of him is to insult me. Must I use the strap again?'

The Rhenish wine was excellent and the Count had them bring across a large leather suitcase, which he opened. Inside were scores of photographic prints. There were all sorts – landscapes, run of the mill stuff, but mostly nudes, nudes in profusion.

'I love women more than anything else. No matter whether they're vulgar or refined, lewd or chaste. I like to pose them in a landscape. To tap their sensual potential and juxtapose the chosen panorama or the appropriate decor . . .'

'You're a connoisseur of the erotic,' I said.

And I continued feasting my eyes on all those fixed moments of femininity, those instants of sensuality revealed and recaptured, those frozen fragments of hotly voluptuous delight.

As night was drawing on, he persuaded me to stay for dinner. The meal proved superb. Then he suggested we watch some blue movies. In the dimmed light and the stifling heat a screen was unrolled and the film wound on. The first image appeared. Five young women were shown arriving for a fishing party. They were handsome creatures, if on the plump side, and were very likely dancers or chorus girls. Their main occupation consisted of hoisting up their skirts, falling into the water, wringing out their sodden clothes, shedding their underwear and so on, gradually achieving a state of undress. Various closeups drew comparisons between the relative luxuriance or sparseness of the pubic hair covering those five mottes, and allowed one to assess the depth if not the texture of the intercrural areas. A forest warden arrived and the women all ran off in panic. He managed to catch one of them. Tugging up her skirts, he bent her over his knee and thrashed her vigorously. One could thus admire her splendid thighs, which were worthy of a Boucher painting. Under the material, that truncheon of authority, evidently lengthy, hard and implacable, stiffened still further. He then unbuttoned himself and sentenced the victim, after that summary trial, to strokes of a different sort. The execution was duly carried out, with a final shot of the ecstatic faces of both officer and trespasser.

Good Lord, it was Meg de Vallac.

'You will never find these films shown in the usual places where such works are circulated. Nor anywhere else,' my host commented. 'They star only famous actors. Just the elite. Some great names among them, I may say.'

When the lights went down again, I was all too aware of the presence of female limbs curving and intertwining in the darkness, and of silken-haired heads softly lolling against one another. And I could confirm, manually, the considerable similarities between the charms of the models and those of the actresses in the film. The young women also looked as if they were greatly enjoying the projection. It was all meltingly hot and tender. And their hands were skilful and nimble, their mouths warm and expert.

In the morning I was back on terra firma. There was a man taking his mules down along the towpath. On a bend, I turned and looked round. The barge had already disappeared. As I walked away I could not help thinking – although I am no sadist, and mine host was certainly something of a practical joker – how much I should have liked to witness one of his darkly hinted sessions with the strap.

* * *

Let's end with the cinema.

Henri and I wanted to shoot a short film. It was the grim story of the kidnapping of an aristocratic young girl by a gang of crooks, and of her rescue by the son of her father's chauffeur, a poor student she had hitherto spurned.

One scene was to depict the young girl quite naked, but not violated, after being brutally stripped by the gangsters. We had hired a young starlet who was very willing to play nude scenes and be groped a little. But each time we were rehearsing this scene – although the first run-through had been sublime enough – we (the two gangsters, played by myself and a friend), the cameraman and Henri (the poor student, as well as being the director), just could not resist and the whole thing degenerated into an orgy. We must have re-started the scene about a dozen times. Every time the starlet, whose name was Odette, was all set to begin yet again, and every time she let herself be leaped upon by four delirious males. At the end of the third day we decided to call a halt. The starlet was paid royally. And Henri, having bribed the cameraman, absconded with such footage as the latter had managed to shoot, including some really spicy sequences – all those infamous rehearsals of our big scene. I believe that he went ahead, without consulting me, and showed them privately.

So much for the cinema.

8

For years I was friendly with Maurice de Collonges. He was a fascinating man. I thought him something of an adventurer, on the lines of Arsène Lupin. He would sometimes tell me about various love affairs he had had, and they were certainly both extravagant and colourful. At that time when I knew him best I was about twenty-five. He appeared to be my exact contemporary and yet he must have been a good ten years my senior.

One episode he related took place on a beach in Normandy when he was seventeen years old. Assorted rather eccentric ladies were given to strolling along it and indeed to flirting outrageously thereupon, under cover of their canvas or wicker windbreaks. One particular Duchess – an Austrian as I recall – seemed greatly attracted to the youthful Maurice who, accompanied by his parents too often for his own liking, did not much appreciate these seaside outings. Nevertheless, he used to carry around a heavy and expensive camera and tripod, taking numerous photographs. One day the Duchess expressed her desire to be photographed in a bathing costume. The photograph like the lady was well developed and he presented it to the aristocrat a few days later, telling her in plain terms if not without blushing, that he was keen to take a portrait of her in the nude, all thoroughly artistic, of course.

She smiled. She was far from averse to the idea, but declared that it would be impossible in her hotel, while the photograph could not be taken al fresco either because 'one might be disturbed'. But Maurice had already devised his plan. It was agreed that he should arrive on the beach very early in the morning. He would then enter the beach hut the Duchess owned. Then she in turn would arrive whenever it was convenient. It was quite important to make sure the light would be good. He was to tell his parents that he was off for 'a constitutional'. And this was what happened. The next day Maurice, armed with the key to the beach cabin, arrived there and installed his equipment.

It had been arranged that the Duchess would pretend to open the door while he simultaneously opened it from the inside. At eleven a.m. the lady appeared. There they were, shut in together, she wearing an extraordinary and enticing swimsuit. She wished to be photographed in the nude first. For the dumbfounded Maurice, she bared her rounded shoulders, big hips and flaxen bush. She had stockings on, and strange high-heeled shoes laced like espadrilles and on the very borderline of good taste. Like that, almost naked, she was thoroughly alluring. Maurice could not restrain himself. The knowledge that the beach around them was by now swarming with people and that his own distinctly prudish parents were neither far off nor without their suspicions, made his head spin. He felt voluptuously stimulated to sense so many people nearby, surrounding them; so many innocent games in progress; so many abortive flirtations taking place only yards away; all those children playing in the sand and building their first sandcastles; all those conformist people on their best behaviour who would be eager to greet the duchess obsequiously when she emerged.

There was scarcely any need for preliminary caresses. Milady was a fast worker who enjoyed her work, and she also proved a fervent disciple of de Sade's main predilection. As Maurice so neatly put it: 'There was I, Maurice de Collonges, the last scion of a good but very minor family of country gentlefolk, entering the highest aristocracy through the back gate, as it were, making a little diversion by way of Sodom's porthole. But how devilishly velvety she was, how soft, deep and hot, my first Duchess! Bohemian in every sense . . .'

After taking his pleasure and his leave from those superbly cushioned posterior portals, he concentrated upon the Duchess's main entrance, coming and going in that thoroughfare also. Then, panic-stricken by this outrage in the middle of a beach in broad daylight (even though concealed by four thin wooden walls), he turned his talents to capturing the Duchess's charms in photographic form.

'I am not vonting to, not vont . . .' she would repeat, protesting against all Maurice's saucier poses, but she invariably adopted them just the same, continuing the litany of reluctance: 'I not vont, eez not nigh-eez, I not vont.'

'I have never really been an innocent,' Maurice told me. 'In my twelfth year however, my mother, who always seemed to me positively venerable although she had scarcely turned thirty, had a close friend called Mme Bouvry who had attained the vast age of twenty-six. This Mme Bouvry, who was still single and was, I believe, a general's daughter, became my cynosure. She was delightful, truly charming in spite of the age gap between us. She knew how to tell stories and listen to my trivial secrets, and would treat me to cakes on the quiet, bringing me sweets too, every once in a while. In the end, she turned into something of a doting aunt where I was concerned, and a friend as well.

'For reasons that remain somewhat unclear to me, it was arranged that I should sleep overnight at her place. This must have been because so many guests were expected and my own bedroom would necessarily have been requisitioned. She herself lived in a rather small flat comprised of a kitchen, a small sitting-room and

94

a bedroom. I was put to bed at about eight p.m. During the night, Mme Bouvry was accompanied home, she and my mother came into the bedroom to see if I was asleep. They had woken me but I pretended I was still asleep, for it was pleasant to feel oneself being looked at, enjoyable to be surrounded by warmth and sympathetic attention, safe and snug in that large and comfortable bed. The light went out again. Then, quite some time later, I sensed someone returning. The light was not switched on. The room was dark, but I could still distinguish Mme Bouvry's figure. She was undressing, that much I could discern from her movements. Just then a car passed. The building stood on a bend in the road, and owing to its position and angle to the street, passing headlamps often lit up that particular room. They would give the effect of a lingering if far paler light than usual. I caught sight of Mme Bouvry and the vision of her body was so clearly imprinted upon my retina that it seemed as if I were looking at her for a full minute or so. She had turned her back to me and was pulling her petticoat over her head. Of course I could see her naked back, buttocks, thighs. She put on a nightdress finally. I felt the sheets pulled aside, the mattress giving under her weight and then a body stretched out next to mine. Instinctively, and without any ulterior motive, I rolled over towards that companionable warmth, and she greeted me, putting her arms around me. I felt protected, but could not help recalling, even as she was holding me so tenderly, that vision of her nudity. Aroused, I sought a more carnal contact, thrusting my abdomen against Mme Bouvry's warmth and accompanying that advance with some suggestive movements. I mean I did not know then, nor did I understand, that that was what they were. Besides, I scarcely realised what was happening to me. But she, my friend, must have known all too well, for she could feel my diminutive masculinity.

'Yet she did not move away.

"Come on, behave yourself," she whispered in my ear, "and just go to sleep."

'This strange exchange surprised me, and oddly enough I did fall asleep. But I must have woken up again in the night, for I remember noticing that Mme Bouvry's nightdress had ridden up past her hips, remember thinking how white and big (in relation to my own size then) her bottom was. Innocently I tucked my stiffened litle dick just below that dark nice niche, and fell fast asleep again, this time soundly, without going any further. In the morning I was awoken by a Mme Bouvry whom I was still clasping in the same questionable position. Seeing that I was awake she smiled, got out of bed, brushed down her nightdress and, before visiting the lavatory, planted a kiss upon my forehead.

'I should add that this unexpected night in no way damaged our chaste friendship. Yet that friendship did not last long, for Mme Bouvry left for the Midi three or four months later, while

I found myself in the days to come dwelling upon the image of a vanished love.

'I knew my parents kept in touch with Mme Bouvry by letter. Hers always included a pleasant message for me, and I invariably received Christmas and birthday presents from her too. I don't know how it came about, but when I was sixteen she invited me to spend a month's holiday there. She lived near Cerbère, and I travelled down without a moment's hesitation. She came to meet me at the station, surprised to find that I was now so grown up and handsome. She had cooked a good dinner which we ate on the terrace, looking out to sea. I felt completely at ease and happy. We recalled those little secrets, those moments of complicity we had shared, but I was talking of them like an adult whereas she still saw me as a child. At one point she said to me:"Do you remember when you slept at my place?"

'She intended nothing in particular by it, of that I am sure, but I blushed and there was an awkward silence. She broke it by adding:

"You weren't a very good little boy."

"I wasn't a little boy any more."

"That I did notice."

'She laid her hand on my knee and squeezed it affectionately through my light summer trousers.

"We won't discuss it again, you're forgiven."

'But during the first few days things grew steadily worse. The way she talked and the way she would touch me or brush against me, aroused my desire. To hide my feelings I turned sullen, almost perverse, and began to avoid her. She seemed saddened by this.

'One morning she arranged an excursion up the mountain to show me the "delightful little cottage" she had rented there.

'Halfway up a storm broke and we were comprehensively soaked, like drowned rats. On reaching the cottage we had one main objective, to dry ourselves as soon as possible. It was cold inside the house. Fortunately there was an open fireplace and I went to fetch some pieces of wood from an adjoining shed. I returned, lit some twists of paper under a pile of twigs and laid some wood on top. On my return I noticed that Mme Bouvry had begun undressing. She had taken a mattress from the bed and placed it together with some cushions on the hearth a few feet in front of the chimney. She was in her underwear and the fitful beginnings of the fire revealed that the sodden material clung to a body I scarcely recollected but was now pleasurably rediscovering. For she was quite a beauty and still young. She took off the rest of her things in a shadowy corner and re-emerged wrapped in a decidedly transparent curtain which she was trying with scant success to spread about her for decency's sake.

"You go and take off your things too. There's another curtain on the armchair."

'While I undressed I saw her putting her wet clothes nearer the fire, and the sight of some fine silk knickers roused me at once. Then she lay down on the mattress.

"You look like a Roman emperor," she said as I too approached the fire to dry out my clothes.

'I myself thought I looked more like a silly idiot. However, I completed the drying operation, put two more logs on the fire and was about to go back to my corner when she began laughing.

"You can't stay back there in the cold. Come here by me and warm up."

'As she said this, her hands reached to feel the ends of her hair and the curtain, which had been badly tucked in around her, slipped down to reveal one perfectly shaped breast. At the same moment she moved to cross her legs and the change of position also bared her thighs. Was it deliberate provocation? Perhaps not at the start, but she became fortune's accomplice by smiling at me and repeating her invitation to me to come closer. I made up my mind to do so and this time, purposely turning to one side, she repeated that smile, displaying both tempting breasts full and firm as exotic fruits.

"Stretch out beside me."

'I obeyed, my last vestige of embarrassment disappearing. But I still felt rather awkward and ungainly. The fire was warming me now, yet behind me I sensed another kind of heat. A hand was placed upon my shoulder.

"All right?"

"Yes."

'The same hand then moved to my stomach and downwards.

''You've grown a lot, my young friend,'' said Mme Bouvry. ''That's quite obvious.''

'Mortified by my slowness, I turned and clutched her brutally in my arms, getting tangled up in the curtains as I did so. I heard her laugh quite spontaneously and without condescension but it irritated me and I ripped away the screen of net material. Her luxuriant pubis was there waiting: I parted her legs with a sort of animal greed. Impatient, guiding my reddened prick in one quivering fist I plunged into her without further ado. Such brutish fierceness on my part in no way deterred her. She acquiesced fully, arching her back and emitting a moan which betrayed her own desire. I thrust in and out, full tilt, as if trying to split her open; it was like a devil's gallop, some furious race in which I could feel her tremble and weaken. The revelation of my virility, in and through this femininity which softened under my body and its movements, absolutely enthralled me. It was all the more thrilling because this other body joined to mine belonged to the respectable lady of my childhood, to my favourite storyteller, my pure love. The performance ended in a blaze of glory, as, warmed by my own heat, she too seemed to find relief. She collapsed upon the mattress, lying there in my arms.

'We stayed in the cottage a good three hours more, but I was gentler.

'You can well imagine how the rest of that

holiday went. Utter exhaustion. As the days passed, however, I fell more and more deeply in love; the more of my very first impressions of her were confirmed, and the more of myself I surrendered.

'When she sat naked she became for me the image of a benevolent deity, that kind if slightly incestuous goddess who soothes childish fears and carries one far away from the dark, threatening forest of the night.

'From her springs I drank nectar, drowsing on scents only sensed in our finest dreams. I remember taking her – her back against my chest, both of us facing the sea – in an other-worldly twilight. The slow friction of our shared flesh gave us a voluptuous feeling of eternity. It was enough to make one weep.'

9

There are recurrent images, born of unforget-
table memories or of vivid dreams. Thus the
image of Maud, undressing in the dark so as to
change and make a rapid return to the nocturnal
garden party, after an accidental drenching in
champagne. I clicked my lighter (or did I light a
match?) and the scene was abruptly illuminated.
She was not in the least scared. Rather, she
tantalized me, standing there like a statue of
glowing flesh sculptured out of the darkness.
She made me a gift of her artlessness. And how
fiery, passionate, soft and moist that artlessness
was! In it I melted in ecstasy.

But isn't this an escapade recounted by
someone else . . .?

Mireille was playing the tambourine at a
Provençal fair. With each whirl of her skirt, she
showed flashes of delectable lingerie, flounce
and frill. I asked her over to my villa, to come
and play her instrument for me alone. She was

sixteen, with dark Andalusian eyes. She also, and equally well, played the fife.

Mme de Landry was waiting for me one summer afternoon in her garden, which was surrounded by high walls. She was a confirmed naturist, and adhered to this cult assiduously. I did not need much convincing, especially since there was no one else at home. Sitting on a sunwarmed bench, she provoked in me thoughts that were less naturist than natural. I possessed her as she crouched over this bench, my knees seeking purchase on the scalding hot stone.

The scent of flowers was making love with the song of the birds.

We had gone for a sort of poetic outing, a poetry group day in the countryside. There I met Irène. She was very attractive and thoroughly proper. Around us there was much versifying and poetic discussions about mystical states, nature and even religion. All these would-be rhymers gnawed wormily and unremittingly at whatever was best in life.

Since I had nothing to lose and only, perhaps, a slap to gain – but one delivered by such a hand! – I leaned over to the very beautiful and reserved Irène, who was listening politely to all these pretentious poetasters, and murmured:

'Mademoiselle, would you like to be buggered naked in a field of flowers?'

She consented. Evidently a lover of real poetry.

My friend Paul's widow was wearing black lingerie. I tore these items off her and she wept in my arms as if ashamed of the feeble token defence she had put up.

To continue on a poetic note: I did wonder then, not about 'snows' or No's, but where indeed were the weeds and evil deeds of yesteryear . . .

One winter evening I had just thrown Paul Géraldy out and was about to bore myself thoroughly, sitting in a stupor in front of a very good wood fire, when there was a knock on the door. It was that fat actress Meg de Vallac. She was fat, but far from ugly. She let an icy draught in with her and gave me a cool yet bracing peck on the cheek. I felt hotter already when she came in. Doffing the big cloak which completely enveloped her, she revealed that she had nothing on underneath it except for a sheer petticoat. That surprised me. She did not remove her hat. 'I want you to photograph me just like this!' she said.

I asked no questions and went ahead, complying with her request. My appetite was aroused by what I saw between the embroidered lace hem of her petticoat and the tops of her stockings. That was the area I longed to bite.

When I had taken enough pictures in the style she wanted, she turned round, bent over to display her rear view, and pulling up the petticoat, remarked while I regaled myself with this impressive spectacle of her nudity: 'My turn to take you!'

And she flashed again, this time capturing a distinctly sodomitical pose . . .

My father, mother, uncle, my new aunt and myself set off for a picnic. Why, at that particular moment, did I go back to the cars? Why was my uncle's young wife perched on the bonnet of one of them, sitting there cradling her knees? Why did she smile at me? Why was her whole attitude somehow not proper?

Ought I to stare at those slender thighs and those all too visible embroidered knickers? But then my uncle arrived and I averted my eyes.

That little Italian woman glimpsed through an open door at the end of an alley. One of the straps of her petticoat had slipped off her shoulder. The dark pink flower of the breast bloomed against the matt skin. Her stockings sheathed the curves of perfect thighs.

I dreamed one night that my mother was going

out to do some shopping. She asked me what I wanted. I was very small, very shy. I experienced an overwhelming onset of desire when I observed she was about to go out into the street, to be seen there by all those men, and with only her scarf, bag, stockings and hat. She was smiling at me. I felt ashamed of myself, and I would have liked to see more, but the dream ended with her turning to open the door – a moment longer and I should certainly have been dazzled by the close-up of her legs and what lay between.

10

I was drawn to Spain, and inevitably I found myself living there for more than a year. The beauty of the landscape moved me, although for a long time I preferred the interiors of the houses. At that period of my life, however, I probably needed a change of scene. For a whole fortnight I frequented the red-light area of Barcelona. During this stay in Spain I also visited different towns and their brothels. There was nothing very distinctive about them.

However, I did have two adventures worth recalling. It is true that like all such memorable encounters they happened to me without my having to look for or initiate them.

I was in an obscure market town that had been baked white under an oven-hot blue sky. I was resting awhile on a small, quiet square, alone. A young woman dressed in black came up to me.

'*Estranjero*?' she inquired, tilting her chin momentarily in the Mediterranean interrogative manner.

I nodded.

'Could you do me a service?' she asked in Spanish, guessing that I understood the language a little.

'Yes.'

She described a tortuous and rather strange itinerary, but in a way which would have led any passerby to think that she was merely informing me rather than arranging a sort of rendezvous. Then she left. I gave her the quarter of an hour she had requested before setting off to meet her again. I wandered through the maze of tiny steeply sloping alleyways, following an ancient town wall like a rampart until I was out of the town centre and walking along a kind of donkey track. The idea that I might be set upon and robbed did cross my mind at one point, but I was feeling adventurous that day and continued on my way. If I were attacked somewhere, at least I had very little money on me.

I reached a kind of suburb on the very outskirts and there in a silent, deserted street, I heard someone call to me in a low voice. I turned round to see my Spanish woman standing in a doorway and gesticulating that I should discreetly rejoin her. I did so and she locked the door behind us. Then we went down a long corridor, and into a cellar, re-emerging in another corridor. She opened a door and when I had entered the room with her she double-locked it. It was very dark. Again, I thought for a moment that I was going to be attacked, but she lit a candle. By its fitful illumination I saw

110

her take off her mantilla before undoing her dress. I smiled to myself, wondering if this could be a new style of prostitution: 'Can you do me a service?' – but in reverse as it were. The approach was certainly original, and the theatrical buildup with its exotic decor had quite won me over: I felt excited. The young woman now resembled something out of *Carmen*, but she was not in the least vulgar. She gazed at me proudly and the scent of the carnation in her hair wafted into my nostrils. She wore a pair of white knickers trimmed with lace, which still concealed her secret, but between the lace hem and her black stockings the soft, rounded flesh seemed to glisten in the shadow.

'Finish undressing me, if you want. And make me come . . . Make me come!'

For a moment or two longer I admired this vision. Then I approached her, somehow managing to contain a feverish desire which she too must have shared, for she gasped slightly when I touched her. Both of us, however, played at remaining cool, calm and collected. Perhaps she was expecting more from me than I knew how to give her? She seemed extremely anxious, I thought, and that led me to believe that she was no prostitute – or at any rate, not a professional. I slipped down her knickers, then felt and weighed and palped the splendid rondure of her flanks. My hands revelled in exploring the smooth contours of those twin globes. As she twisted and wriggled her body in order to help me divest her completely of her underwear she repeated:

111

'Make me come!'

She was gasping loudly. I think I succeeded well enough in doing her the service which she had requested of me, for she blazed quickly and fiercely, like a long-banked fire suddenly stoked and fanned by wind to a scorching intensity.

After this erotic banquet dominated by her big, beautiful Iberian buttocks, I was none the wiser as to whether I should offer any payment. I did not do so, probably because I sensed she was neither a loose woman nor a whore, but a neglected wife, a sensual woman oppressed by the harsh rituals of her country. Too newly wed for motherhood, and too cautious to take a lover who for her would resemble all the others – a Spaniard, that is – she had selected a random foreigner like myself.

I count myself lucky, and feel I must have acquitted myself well, for I later read that an Englishman had been found half-naked and stabbed, in one of the disused cellars in that very same town. The crime was ascribed to thieves. My guess is that it had more to do with pride nettled by a payment, with sensuality derided and with *a service ill-performed*.

'Do you know Casarès?' said Don Felipe.

Disturbed, for I was admiring a very neatly turned out Spanish woman bather on a little beach at Estepona, I replied nonetheless:

'No.'

'Let's go then!'

Don Felipe was doing exactly as he pleased, taking things easy. As for myself I did not really want to miss the rest of the show.

'I'll have the horses saddled and we'll get going.'

And how! That wretched fellow did look after his guests well, but he hardly gave them a chance even to think for themselves. I was accordingly committed to a sore arse for fifteen miles or so up in the Ronda mountains. Off we went, and after following the spectacular coastal route for a while we took a smaller path that led up into the mountains. After a few miles I had tired of praising a landscape that was almost too breathtaking, and was wondering if I would ever reach Casarès in one piece. Perhaps my horse, hitherto docile, might yet succeed in breaking my back, or Don Felipe despatch me with a blow of his *navaja* if I complained. We branched off, however, and I realised that we were heading straight up the mountain.

'Where are we going?' I asked, trying to suppress a groan. 'Are we still bound for Casarès?'

'No, we'll be arriving there later, probably tomorrow.'

Then where were we going? To get ourselves killed, or to camp out like gypsies?

'It's a surprise,' Don Felipe declared, smiling.

I said nothing more. For a long time we traversed impossible tracks, until we finally reached a hacienda or something very like one. It was situated in the hollow of a small valley

like an amphitheatre. An arroyo, miraculously
not dried up, flowed past the house, which was
imposing and had obviously cost money. On
our approach a man armed with a rifle leaped
out from behind a rock. He looked distinctly
unfriendly but when he recognised Don Felipe
he grinned. There was an exchange of courtesies
in the Andalusian dialect. Then we dismounted.
I noted to my amazement that I could still stand
up straight. A pair of heavy wooden doors
studded with nails opened and we entered the
hacienda. In the darkness under the archway I
observed another man armed with a rifle.

'Who are these people, the descendants of
Jose-Maria's bandits?'

Don Felipe guffawed. A man, apparently
unarmed, but with deep pouches to his trousers
that might well have concealed a long knife or
even a revolver, hurried to stable our horses. I
followed my host, who was crossing the huge
tiled courtyard. Where was I? Was this some
exclusive and particularly expensive brothel?
After passing through an open porch and
walking down a corridor we emerged onto a
sumptuous patio. We were surrounded by clois-
tered arcades such as one finds in the Genera-
life, while encircling us higher up and beyond
were the mountains. I was, and remained,
astounded by this setting. The courtyard was
even patterned with mosaics made from tiny
round pebbles or shingle, black, white and pink,
arranged to form arabesques and other motifs.
It was cool, for a great fountain with four criss-

crossing jets of water played in the centre. Soon I caught sight of a young woman lying on a chaise longue, reading, in the cloister. We moved towards her.

'Donna Isabella,' Don Felipe said very simply by way of introduction.

She put out her hand, smiling. She had been reading Proust, *Un Amour de Swann*, in the original. She rose to her feet and in her company we toured most of the house, whose furnishings were truly extraordinary. Her French was very good. I realised that she was both well-bred and well-educated. She invited us to stay the night.

The meal was good, and I particularly enjoyed the ham and the local wine. When dinner was over she announced that she would dance for us in the gipsy style. She left us for some time, returning in the costume of a *gitanilla* from Granada. Her dance was punctuated rhythmically by her castanets and the guitar music drifting through from another room. I thought to start with that the music came from a gramophone. Don Felipe informed me that it did not and that there was a professional guitarist living on the premises. It was not at first clear to me why she did not want him nearer her. She danced very well, in a wild possessed fashion. I noticed that like myself Don Felipe was more than impressed: he too was aroused. She stopped. The dim light lent her face a strange radiance. She seemed remote, detached, yet at the same time sexually stimulated. She left the room but quickly returned, and it proved quite

115

a shock. She had on only a mantilla, a very transparent one too. Then she swept it off with a sort of naive perversity, quite shamelessly displaying herself before us.

'Would you like me to dance naked or with my mantilla?'

Since we did not reply she began dancing again, worked herself up into a frenzy, then flung us the mantilla. Our dry throats were in dire need of more alcohol, so we saw to it that we had even more to drink. Finally she stopped dancing and laughed dementedly. She ran to a chair and sprawled across it in a thoroughly lecherous manner, shouting:

'I'm the biggest whore in Spain, come on and fuck me!'

It was true that her pink and crinkly private folds proved tempting indeed . . .

Next morning we mounted up and set off again for Casarès.

'Incredible!' I said, to break the early morning stillness.

Don Felipe looked at me and smiled.

'Do you know why she's like that?' he said. 'She is the daughter of a Spanish grandee. One day she happened to see a gypsy woman dancing in a village square. Who knows what instincts the sight awakened in her . . .? She had the urge to learn how to dance in that style and to see more of such dancing. She pestered her major-domo until he agreed to take her, disguised, secretly and by night, to a sleazy dive. The wild dances of the gypsies and the other women astonished and fascinated her; all those violent and sexually stimulated males around her drove her crazy with desire. On their return the major-domo, also aroused to fever pitch, and aware that she might be available, took advantage of her. When he had regained his senses, he then tried to strangle her in order to cover up the original crime. She survived, but on her recovery she wanted to give herself to all the male servants in the household. Her father had her confined.'

'So she's a sick woman,' I said.

'In a way. She's very young, you know. She was raped at the age of thirteen.'

A German friend had invited me to stay with him. He lived in Berlin, in a comfortable flat which he shared with several mistresses. When I went over there, none of them were in occupation, of course. But the stay was very pleasant. He took me along to various dives, some of them low and rough, others exclusive and dull. Yet in the evenings whenever we set off for an unknown destination – he adopting his usual air of mystery – I would spend the whole journey fantasising that the establishment to which he was taking me would at least prove to be of above average interest. Prior to then I'd had occasion to sample a few German women, but they were more often seasoned professionals on the Voyage to Cythera – if I may put it thus – than enthusiastic amateurs.

The car stopped by some railings which fenced in what looked like park grounds. The gates were opened, or rather half-opened, for us. My friend Hans had to display a piece of paper before the armed watchman finally opened the heavy wrought-iron gates wide. The limousine slid forward into the dark tunnel of a long and imposing avenue of tall trees. We went on for perhaps half a mile more until a huge and brightly lit house appeared. A footman, dressed rather like a verger, came and held open the car doors. He asked Hans for his number. Hans produced a kind of token upon which a large number '15' was engraved. The footman thanked him and escorted us inside. We entered a room that was obscurely lit – in fact in semi-darkness – and sat down at one of the tables. We were asked whether we wished to eat or simply required drinks. I was hungry and ordered the best, whatever was the speciality of the house. Actually it was very good indeed. Yet my initial impression persisted: for all the palaver about the armed guard, the flunkey, the special membership number and so on, I ranked this place along with others in the category of 'exclusive, snobbish or boring', and in this particular instance I even added the adjective 'pretentious'.

I let Hans into some of my criticisms and he accepted them without demur, with even a slightly superior smile.

'Wait a bit,' he said.

I did wait. I picked up snatches of conversations here and there: these were either stilted, highflown or pro-National Socialist. I lay low. Finally two more flunkeys began placing candelabra with three or four candles apiece upon every table. I could now see the whole room. It was crowded – a hundred or maybe a hundred and twenty people at about forty tables. The high society set: aristocracy and the wealthy upper middle class.

Nothing much happened after the sudden illumination, except that four young women dressed as ballerinas appeared. One of them soon made her way over to us. She curtsied to us briefly.

'Good evening gentlemen,' she said. 'Have you agreed to take part in our little game?'

'Naturally,' said Hans.

'In that case, green, yellow, blue, red or white?' she asked me.

I hesitated, then said: 'Blue.'

She gave me a small counter, painted blue. Hans chose red. She was about to turn away when Hans called her back.

'This gentleman is French and this is his first time here. Could you kindly do up your sandal?'

I had scarcely cottoned on: indeed, I was somewhat bewildered. The young woman, who bore more than a passing resemblance to my friend the actress Helena Junebelle (Helga Jungblut), rivalling the latter's buxom charms, so that I recalled Helena-Helga herself with a hot

119

twinge of desire, obeyed him, bending over so she was at my eye-level. As her tutu tilted up, a pair of round, firm buttocks were exposed to view, and the sudden crude proximity of these very creditable cruppers, together with the excellent and thoroughly alcoholic repast, suffused my own cheeks with a deep and obvious blush.

'It's quite in order to have a feel,' Hans remarked.

I hesitated, but Hans insisted. I dared not look about me for I felt myself the cynosure of the whole room. Anyhow, I did have a quick and furtively hypocritical glance around the nearest tables. I thus assured myself that these staid army officers in mufti, and diplomats in evening dress, those lawyers and doctors – even the ones accompanied by various ladies or by their wives – did not eschew the opportunity to flick up the short skirts, with lecherous grins at that, not to mention some distinctly indecent comment. Certain of the women present laughed uproariously, as if they would have liked to change places with the bogus dancers. My embarrassment immediately vanished, therefore, and with a drunk's feigned innocence I briskly groped that full, pink and white and very Aryan arse, even sneaking my hand betwixt and between to feel Tannhauser's grotto where the blond heroes were engendered.

This little interlude lasted a good half-hour, and I no longer regretted my presence there. I now understood why everyone in the place was so patient, and by the end of the evening I was to understand still better. There followed an oppressive, expectant hush, until at last a heavy velvet curtain was drawn apart to reveal an illuminated rostrum. Below it, in the darkness, musicians had noiselessly taken their places – or had they been there all along? With studied reverence they played Wagner. As soon as the music stopped, a tall, rather handsome man of about fifty appeared on the dais.

'Ladies and gentlemen, I give you: the Führer!'

The whole room stood, everyone's right arm extended in salute. I rose too, bowed slightly, but did not raise my arm. Luckily for me, no one held that against me.

'Ladies, gentlemen,' he continued when we were all seated again, 'we will now let you know the result of our little draw.'

Taking his time and playing the suspense for all it was worth, he flourished a scrap of paper.

'Table fifteen.'

Every eye was upon us.

'And it's . . . blue.'

That was myself.

'What have I won?' I whispered to Hans.

'You'll see,' he replied.

'The gentleman is French, I believe,' the man went on. 'We shall ask him to select a lady from among those present. Whichever one he prefers.'

'Then what?' I asked my friend, seeking some sort of confirmation.

'Go ahead,' he said.

I scanned the audience and soon spotted my prey. She was an unusually elegant woman, and I had not noticed her laughing loudly or raising her voice, but I had certainly been struck by her reserve and a certain Olympian detachment about her beauty – a haughty awareness of status and power. When it was clear that she had been singled out, she rose gracefully to her feet. I saw her turn pale but I still did not understand why. Those present seemed both pleased and disturbed by the choice.

'Madame,' the man invited her suavely.

The lady moved over to the rostrum. As she passed the musicians she whispered something to one of them. Then she climbed on to the dais and the man made himself scarce. At every table the candles were put out, while the music began playing very softly in the dark. The light on the small makeshift stage dimmed then focused directly and solely upon the lady. She really was a remarkable beauty. At that moment I think I began to understand.

It was very likely she herself who had selected the sublime piece of music that was surely intoxicating us all. I could not help smiling at the thought that when it came to the most scabrous, absurd or appalling aspects of life, the Germans invariably liked to set them to music.

The young woman began to undress with elegant and discreet movements. The room held its breath. She undid the clasps of her long evening gown (I was sorry she was so flimsily clad) and let it slide to the floor. Then she slowly rolled down her stockings, removed her shoes, putting the latter back on when she had finally shed and tossed aside the silk wisps. Her breasts were now exposed and as she stood up straight again I could admire her, albeit with a dry and open mouth, for she was quite simply perfect. She wore fine oyster silk knickers and a sort of long dark petticoat which she skilfully tied behind her neck; with her breasts and pubic area hidden behind this improvised screen she slipped her knickers down her long slim thighs. When she stepped out of the material and kicked it to one side, she maintained a pose of extraordinary and exquisite grace, smiling to herself a smile which seemed to reflect an eternal youth. She gave a little sign and the music ceased.

In an awesome silence she turned her back to us, revealing a rear view to drive anyone crazy, before very gradually turning to face us again. She untied the knotted material and that too fell. For one brief moment her blonde triangle and the outline of the cleft were visible. Then the light went out. All one could discern were a few quick movements on the dais. A filtered light returned, permeating the room, and the music recommenced.

No one was talking. I observed the table at which the lady I selected had been sitting. She was not back there yet. In the end I said to Hans: 'Is this the usual routine? Who is that woman? And why was I chosen?'

'Not so many questions at once. This kind of dinner takes place only once a week. All the Berlin upper crust come here. To hot things up, they have these sorts of goings on. Seats are expensive – I've succeeded in getting in only a couple of times before.'

'But do the women have to submit to taking their clothes off?'

'By coming here they run the risk of having to do so. That's precisely what spices up the evening. And as you probably guessed, many of them are waiting solely for that. To rile their lover, husband, fiancé. Or quite simply to exhibit themselves in front of wellbred, elegant males who in their turn will misbehave and wet their immaculate trousers.'

'Can't the draws be rigged in advance? Isn't there the chance someone might cheat?'

'In Germany one doesn't cheat,' Hans said emphatically.

I was silent. The man from the rostrum headed towards us. He greeted us with a very aristocratic bow, then, turning to myself, remarked: 'According to the general custom, the lady would normally have to come to your table to spend time in conversation. Could you forgo that? She is counting on your sense of honour. She would prefer to leave now.'

'It's a pity,' I said, 'but I agree. Please convey my compliments. And also my sheer admiration.'

He thanked me and left. When I turned towards Hans again, I could see only too well that he seemed highly uneasy. But I could get nothing out of him while the show continued. The four ballerinas had appeared onstage and, still virtually knickerless, proceeded to dance – artistically enough – extracts from well-known ballets. The overall effect was indecent and wildly exciting.

After the evening ended, Hans agreed to talk to me, yet he still seemed rather reticent.

'You are a foreigner, which is why you were able to pick out that particular young woman. None of us would have done so.'

I could find out nothing further. Was she some famous actress, or the wife, mistress or daughter of some bigshot in the Reich? I did not know. But it is a riddle which to this day remains an exquisite torment to me.

HAVE SURPRISE FOR YOU STOP ran the telegram from my friend Robert Martinet, who is both explorer and painter when the mood takes him: HURRY STOP INCREDIBLE.

On the subject of Robert Martinet, here's a story about the time we were in Italy. It was in Venice, and began with a poverty-stricken young lad coming up to us in a narrow alley.

'Do the signori like to see fine pictures, pretty signoras?'

We were under no illusions: fine pictures of pretty ladies had to mean the proverbial etchings, lurid ones at that. I myself had had a surfeit of sun, while Robert needed some distraction, since his young wife had run off with a lover and he had received no further news of any kind. So we dupes followed our youthful pimp. He led us into an even more wretched quarter of town. (Poverty in certain Latin countries seems to outdo itself: there invariably exists a district even poorer than the one you are in.) We were taken across a courtyard swarming with shouting mommas and bawling kids.

'The good life, eh,' Robert remarked.

I couldn't manage a smile. We climbed a staircase and our guide knocked on one of the doors. We heard furniture and chairs being moved around. A moment later a voice asked in Italian:

'Who is it?'

'Enrico,' our lad told him.

The door was opened.

'Come in, gentlemen.'

He was quite a handsome young man, whose face showed considerable character. The room, though cluttered, was clean, and it contained an amazing profusion of nudes. Enrico slipped away after Robert had discreetly tossed him a coin.

'I speak French,' the man said, 'if you'd prefer.' When we nodded, he continued: 'I studied in Paris.'

Then he showed us his paintings of women. The best of it was that he turned out to be an excellent artist. His style was very detailed and he painted with rare precision and, when he pleased, also with poetry, humour and a highly sophisticated eroticism. We were quite taken with his work. We selected from all his various styles, ranging from the fine to the most obscene. He had consented as we were 'knowledgeable collectors' to show us 'exclusively' his special portfolio of erotica. This was comprised of couples, trios, groups, and all kinds of orgies, some involving dogs, donkeys, goats, sheep and other animals. It was obsessive and fiendish, almost insane. We were sickened by it and yet filled with a kind of amazed, reluctant admiration. We did buy a few smaller canvases which struck us as brilliantly scabrous, and then he suggested we watched him at work painting his current model. We agreed and he knocked on a door concealed by a curtain. He paused before opening it and beckoned us to precede him. We entered and had an immediate dazzling vision of a woman, naked except for her stockings and shoes, displaying her back, buttocks and thighs. She was leaning against the artist's easel. She turned round.

'Hélène!' cried Robert.

It was his wife.

Anyhow, I set off to see Robert without further delay. His flat on the Ile Saint-Louis was enormous and needed to be, for it housed a vast assortment of everything he had brought back with him from his expeditions. It was a real hotchpotch of the finest and most appalling items. He welcomed me with a big smile, slapping me on the back.

'You got the telegram, then?'

'So what's it all about?' I asked.

'Hold your horses, will you? Calm down and have a bit of patience! Let's take it easy, eh?'

'All right, but do spill the beans . . .'

But he was not keen to do so immediately. He dragged me into the drawing room and made me imbibe some truly awful variety of rotgut. Then I was taken on a guided tour of various rooms in which he had stored the illgotten gains from his latest trip. I had already observed that he was carefully avoiding the bedroom, his favourite room, where he usually kept his rarest trophies and assorted souvenirs of his youth. He prevailed upon me to smoke a havana before he was willing even to mention his surprise. Exasperated, I urged him in no uncertain terms to get a move on.

'Come on, show me what's in the bedroom. I'm absolutely agog! And running out of patience!'

'You'll spoil half my fun.'

'That's no reason. And anyhow, you've achieved the desired effect — I'm at the end of my tether.'

'Right, you oaf, follow me!'

He opened the bedroom door for me and there she was, sitting on the hearth; I saw her reflection first, in the mirror. She was naked but for a sort of turban. She had the figure of a goddess, with the prettiest breasts I'd ever seen. In her, sex and fecundity, youth and maturity, seemed to meet.

'My slave,' said Robert.

'You're joking,' I replied in astonishment.

'No, I bought her in an Arabian town where I had the necessary contacts and could do so on the quiet. She's Lebanese. Come and see how beautiful she is. She belongs to me body and soul.'

The old devil was exultant.

'You can touch, feel how firm and resilient she is. Sweet and wholesome too. Guess how old she is.'

'Twenty.'

'Just sixteen, old chap.'

He urged me to part her thighs, so I could see for myself, as he put it. And he gave me permission to penetrate her with my finger and to caress her breasts and bottom.

'You're a real friend,' he said, 'and I don't think there's a better way of honouring one's best friend.'

I stayed until very late that night. She performed a strange sort of belly dance for us and consented to our every whim. As I left Robert's, I told myself that it was shameful that slavery still existed . . . Yet I would greatly have liked to possess a young woman like Aicha. Unlike Robert, though, I don't think I'd have shared her with anybody. Egoist I may have been, but I was also more tender and respectful towards women.

A slave was certainly exhilarating, all the same!

11

I felt in a playful mood, and instructed the proprietress of a certain excellent establishment that I wished to organise a little fetishistic entertainment. I've always found knickers (especially of the old-fashioned split variety) and slips, petticoats and women's underwear in general, highly stimulating, and I was glad to have the opportunity of recreating a few welcome surprises I had experienced and which were due largely to lingerie of one kind or another.

Hélène, a sweet young girl of about twenty, and an inmate of that particular house in Normandy, where her main speciality was to offer affection to elderly gentlemen, assumed for me the persona of a pleasant maidservant I once undressed years ago, while her mistress was keeping me waiting overlong.

The little tart was wearing a sort of culotte belonging to her employer, which spectacularly became her. My fingers fluffed out its lace trim and then moved on to grip and stroke the velvet it concealed – which was indeed hers alone, along with those moist and crinkled silks. While she moaned in her throes, the mistress of the house at last appeared and uttered a loud exclamation herself. She rushed at me and the maid too, demanding that the latter return her property at once. This to such good effect that my little maid (who had doubtless foreseen the whole thing) gave her back simultaneously both apron and knickers. I had had the additional impudence to stay where I was throughout this scene and the maid's final action delighted me. I immediately offered her a position on my own staff.

I was a gentleman, after all.

'Simone,' I said, 'you usually dress up in a blouse and white socks, with ribbons in your hair when you're playing little schoolgirls who need spanking. Would you now be the perverse pupil who obliged me when I was in her company – and I was then an old buffer of forty – to fumble her lace frills?'

The window in her tiny room was open and we were listening to the children playing below. You kicked your legs like a mad thing, flailing out of your minimal shirt. Your pose was that of a baby, the family photographing you for posterity. I photographed you for posteriority. And, of course, like a loving mamma, I embraced your precocious baby's bottom.

Its cheeks smelt splendidly of soap.

* * *

Don't pretend to be so surprised, Madame Etienne! You were waiting for me to come in at just this moment. Yes, you, the wife of my father's Manager. You were wearing a delightful petticoat. What's that you say? I shouldn't have looked? Oh, come off it! Oh, it *is* coming off. What a superb outfit your bare skin is.

Who was that little Lorette, up-ended in an attic room of a provincial theatre? What part was she rehearsing when I surprised her? Clad all in Second Empire lace and readily available upon the lifting of her crinoline, she parted her legs in their modest young lady's pantaloons most immodestly, thus offering me the dark moss over the open promise of an almost wild flower. I was grateful to her while I delved inside her with my tongue, seeking a delicate juice she willingly dispensed with parted lips.

Yolande, from Normandy, expert milker of men, performed that service either gloved or bare-palmed; with a sponge in the bath, or squatting, skirts hoisted, atop a bidet so as to catch in the folds of her fine pinafore the spurts of male seed. She it was who wished to let me taste her cunt's linctus and dressed up as Eugenie de Montijo, what's more, so that I could relive visually, photographically and carnally that long-lost scene. Her flower (all too service-able, alas!) had by no means the same savour as that of my petite actress.

I'm sure of that.

* * *

You were beautiful, nameless one! Paris was being jostled into spring when I found myself hiding in a stranger's bedroom, stealing saucy photographs. Who had let me in there . . . ? You were getting ready for some special occasion or other. Eager to look your best. Strewing silken nests of your underwear here and there, sliding each item smoothly on only to hurl it brutally away. Your two tiny breasts seemed to shine, translucent and fragile. I could see your entire thigh, almost all one buttock emerge from the frothing lace. But you were proper as well as beautiful. And if I did not manage to glimpse your downy niche, at least your armpit provided some compensation. My liquid lust would have filled it neatly. You discovered me, however, and a cry escaped your lips.

As I had to escape you.

'A woman has the importance of a nest between two branches,' said Jules Renard. And you, Rolande, my love of just one evening, encountered on a train, you sheathed those twin branches in lace. At your nest I pecked, finding there a tender little beak which swelled and swelled. I used that nest, and also another smaller one, higher or lower according to the position.

You were by no means displeased, despite your denials and expostulations, which seemed to imply that I ought not to have entered there.

* * *

Lace of farewell, shaken in the sooty breeze of a railway station. Under the vast glass and metal marquee keeping track of sighs, smiles, promises. Under the Marquise also, there was lace. Of noble variety.

Lace whose encrusted tracks skimmed Sodom, and Gomorrah too, and paradise lost and found, and that dark forest of childhood tales. Whoever infiltrates, sinks, adheres. Sweat makes it the more intimate.

Madame Durand, your corset was laced tight, your whole attitude was lax, relaxed. You were kneeling beside a bedroom chair, praying by what lay ritual, what diabolic rite? Your very presence was depraved. Your knickers had sunk deep and taut into the cleft between your buttocks. An alarming way of showing me your under and inbetween wear. Naturally you had upon your head your respectable lady's bonnet, but you also wore an impertinent little guttersnipe's smile. And before ravishing you thoroughly I spanked you.

12

Maurice de Collonges and myself had sat down at a table in one of the smarter Parisian cafés, when we saw a lady who had just emerged from the toilets pass our table. She looked highly respectable and was evidently relieved; she eyed us both with a somewhat scornful air. We were surprised at that, but not in the least shocked; women who have recently pulled down their panties often assume this lofty demeanour on their return from performing a perfectly natural function. The fact would have gone unremarked had not another young woman then emerged from the basement. As she came up the stairs she too – though there was something at once distraught, fearful and furtive about her – tried, in brushing past us, to adopt that same casual yet rather haughty manner.

'So, we've been admiring our little pussy in the porcelain, have we? You naughty creature!'

The young woman blushed, hurrying for the exit. Now that might have been that, we'd simply have had a good laugh – except that I happened to see the first lady meet the second on the pavement outside. They then left in each other's company. I pointed this out to Maurice, who started laughing.

'I bet they did more than piss.'

'What do you mean?'

'Well, old man, I've an inkling they had something of a mutual fondle, and that apart from gazing at their pussies in the bowl they stroked them till the tears came. I'm positive!'

He reflected for a moment, then sprang to his feet and rushed out of the café, going up to a young paper-seller.

'I'll buy the lot, dear boy, but I'd like you to do something for me. You see those two ladies over there. Follow them and don't let them out of your sight. Make a note of where they live. If they separate, follow the taller one in the grey hat. Right? We'll wait here for you. This is for your newspapers. You'll get three times as much if you bring us back some good information.'

We went back in and sat down. Maurice was rubbing his hands. I was quite intrigued.

'The bet's not on yet. But the hare is started. You see, if that first woman in the grey hat hadn't irritated us, and if the shorter one hadn't looked so disconcerted and – did you notice? – not very well off for all her studiedly fashionable clothes, nothing would have happened. Have you been to this place often before?'

'Oh, two or three times perhaps.'

'I've been here about a dozen times I suppose. Anyhow, the scene we've just witnessed reminded me of another. I thought I remembered the woman in the grey hat. I was sitting at a pavement table then. She came and sat down for about as long as it takes to settle a bill. Another woman, who must also have just emerged from the toilets, was dawdling on the pavement. The woman in the grey hat then got up and rejoined her. I can only have recorded that particular scene subconsciously, since the two women doubtless struck me as attractive and somehow conspiratorial also. It was the similarity to today's episode which jogged my memory. I may be mistaken, but a friend once talked to me about this café. He said it was a haunt of beautiful females looking for others. Very likely young working-class girls, personable ones tired of their hard-earned pittance, come here to indulge in some genteel prostitution . . . without the risk of pregnancy.'

Listening to Maurice, I thought back to the lovely friends of my youth, Mme Chartier and Mlle Janvier, and once again I seemed to see their secret depravities which that uncle of mine had captured for a short posterity.

We carried on talking about this and that, but both of us were restless and impatient. It was almost seven p.m., more than an hour and a half later, when our young newsboy came in, very pleased with himself. The barman scowled at him and was about to chase him out when he saw him heading towards us, whereupon he retreated behind his counter. The lad sat down confidently.

'I could really do with a beer,' he announced.
We smiled at this gentle piece of blackmail
and bought him one.

'I know where they hang out. Passy. They led
me quite a dance in the end, but lucky for me
they walked there.'

'What number and which road?'

'Rue du Ranelagh.'

He told us the number too. And he drank the
beer in great gurgling gulps, a knowing look
in his eye. He was obviously about to venture
something else, picking his moment. He put
down his glass, then clicked his tongue.

'She's well-known.'

Then he stopped, enjoying keeping us in
suspense.

'I even know the floor and the flat.'

We congratulated him loudly and he became
quite smug.

'I went in and the concierge chucked me out.
Told me the service stairs were at the side. Fine
I said, but I have to deliver a parcel for the lady
who just went up and I've got to know which
floor. Ah, you mean Mme Serre, she tells me
with a bloody plum in her mouth. Third, left
hand side. Right, says I, and took off. So, you've
even got the name, see?'

We said nothing for a moment or two; fine
vistas of possibility opened up ahead of us.

'Look here, do you intend to sell newspapers
all your life? Or would you rather help produce
them? How old are you?'

'Fifteen. Yes, if possible.'

'Could be you're in luck – tomorrow. I'll write you a letter of introduction to a newspaper editor I know. So get ready to become a new Hearst. Here's what I owe you, plus a bonus for the lady's name, which wasn't included in our deal.'

Overjoyed, the lad pocketed his reward, thanked us casually, and put out his hand, which we had no compunction about shaking.

'I like cunning, resourceful types,' Maurice said on his departure. 'They always come in useful.'

He rubbed his hands once more and added:

'I'm now almost certain Mme Serre treats herself to a assortment of young meat, pussy of the year, etcetera. Yes, definitely.'

'I am, too,' I said.

And I had a vision of laces and silks crumpled or slithering off or being opened, revealing jet-black clumps and purple-lipped clefts, full white thighs set off by black stockings and colourful fancy suspenders. Of prying hands insinuating themselves into damp, slippery rippling sphincters; of women's lips meeting and their lower lips rubbing together; of softly rounded breasts tipped with brown or pink nipples crushed against one another.

'Mme Serre is our quarry,' exclaimed Maurice as he rose to his feet.

I followed him into the night which had just fallen. Half an hour later we were in Rue du Ranelagh. We climbed upstairs without hesitation or being intercepted by any mean old con-

cierge who bullied the poor. We reached the
third floor and knocked. After a long pause we
had to knock again. Finally we heard footsteps.
She answered – and she had obviously been
disturbed in the midst of her frolics.

'Who's that?' a voice inquired from behind the
heavy door.

'Are you Madame Serre?'

'Yes.'

'Madame Serre, we are your punishment!
Your sins have found you out and you will soon
be punished for them.'

We heard the woman's sharp intake of breath
and we rushed downstairs. It was only when
we reached the street that we burst out laughing
like schoolboys overcome by their joke in bad
taste.

I have to admit that our first piece of devilry
was sending her a rather wicked letter. It was
laid out in the form of a school textbook ques-
tionnaire, the sort where dots replace the salient
words. For example:

*This lady in a grey hat who is kissing another lady
is a . . .*

*Here they are inside a flat. They are doing things to
each other. They . . . and they . . .*

*Their fingers and tongues are never idle. Mme Serre
greatly enjoys having her clitoris . . .* etc etc.

We advised her to complete the necessary
phrases as indicated and to forward the form to
us, poste restante, at her earliest convenience.
We added too that this was the first exercise in
a long series.

When we never received the completed exercise we sent her a second letter. In this we declared our astonishment at our pupil's lack of application, requesting her to turn up to a specific spot in the Luxembourg Gardens where we looked forward to the pleasure of spanking her in the presence of witnesses. That brought no response either, so we then resolved to visit her at home, to hear her excuses for her lack of enthusiasm in meeting our expectations.

She answered the door and without our even announcing ourselves she turned pale.

'We are the teachers,' Maurice said, 'and we should very much like to know why there was no answer to . . .'

She made a sign to him to lower his voice.

'My husband is in there. Please, I beg you to leave. I'll meet you at the Luxembourg as arranged in two hours' time.'

'We will do as we said,' Maurice whispered.

'Yes, yes,' she said and promptly closed the door.

'Do you think we can get away with it?'

'Of course,' Maurice replied.

I was dumbfounded by his complete confidence. What had he dreamed up?

Mme Serre turned up punctually to the rendezvous, two hours later on the dot.

'What have I ever done to you to make you persecute me so?' she began by asking us.

'Persecute is a rather weighty word. Graver than we had cause to use in relation to yourself. Please recall your arrogant air at the Café X.'

She turned pale.

'Let's move on to serious matters. Follow us.'

We headed for a more isolated area of the Gardens, even less frequented now that it was growing late. But there were still people about. Maurice sat down on a bench and made Mme Serre bend over his knee. We then of course became the centre of attraction. And so the not very respectable old men, the soldiers, the nannies, the mothers with prams, the little scamps who would have their ears boxed for being back home too late, the evening pipe-smokers out for neighbourly strolls – all of them saw my friend's deft gesture as he whisked up Mme Serre's dress to reveal her frilly knickers, and all of them saw him deliver four sharp slaps.

Mme Serre shrieked, thus ensuring that her splendid and outraged rump rippled even more emphatically for being put on general exhibition and thrashed in the bargain. Maurice immediately pulled her to her feet and the three of us strode briskly towards a car whose engine was already running. We dived in and the car moved off. In our wake we could hear assorted shouts of 'Help, thieves!', 'Stop them!' and so forth. The speed of the action had bewildered one and all, while its stylised pictorial quality had perhaps aroused in some of the spectators a certain sensation of complicity.

'Our night is not yet over,' Maurice said. 'We're inviting you to our place.'

Mme Serre protested, but since she knew she

scarcely had a leg to stand on, as it were, she lapsed into silence for the rest of the journey.

Mme Serre had very attractive fair hair. Going against the prevailing fashion of the day, she had left it very long, and it was gathered into a sort of bun at her nape. When she was naked – for she soon saw our logic – we obliged her to kneel. As she was wearing long black gloves and stockings, her skin seemed all the whiter, meet to be beaten maybe. While she knelt, and viewed from the rear, those black stockings formed a sort of plinth upon which rested twin cheeks in the shape of a heart. We made her adopt a variety of unwholesome or suggestive postures for our delectation and I must confess that we masturbated copiously and for the most part upon her.

We drove her back home, taking the precaution of bandaging one of her ankles. Her panic-stricken husband saw us arrive: it was nearly midnight and we were supporting a Mme Serre who was moaning – again, and differently. We explained to him that she had come to grief in a deserted street where, unable to walk, she was also unable to summon help. Fortunately we were passing in our car . . . He thanked us and danced attendance on his wife. We devoutly hoped he would not undress her himself, for we had kept her panties as a souvenir.

There the story of Mme Serre ends.

For myself, however, there was a curious

145

epilogue to it. One night at about ten, I happened to be passing Rue du Ranelagh, on the way back home from a friend's. I saw a very young girl coming out of Mme Serre's building. She was looking to right and left rather furtively before venturing out of the main entrance. On a sudden impulse I hurried to catch her up, although she had begun to increase her pace.

'You've been to Mme Serre's.'

This really startled her.

'I've done nothing wrong,' she said.

'Would you like me to accompany you home and speak to your parents? Or for your employer or the police to know?'

She was trembling.

'What do you want?'

'I'll be reasonable, I'm a nice enough fellow. Just tell me what she did to you.'

She all but jumped out of her skin at that.

'I couldn't.'

'Come on, try a bit harder. You won't be punished for it.'

So she told me everything, in quite modest language except when it came to parts of the body (and doubtless the coarser terms she then used were the only ones she knew), and her story would have inflamed many a libertine. To mention a few details: the moment she arrived at Mme Serre's the latter forced her to crouch on all fours, straddled her, pulled down her drawers and beat her with a whip 'right on the bare bum'. She then made her 'lick her tits and sniff her cunt'. She also stuck her finger up her arsehole, complained the girl, adding that she found this particular action 'sodding disgusting'. A young girl from the slums, she did not understand how the upper classes could be so complicated, so sordid in their loves. She preferred her own crows – young thugs who would not be in the least worried about putting her on the streets one day, when she would have to submit to violently perverted tastes and bourgeois nastiness of every kind.

I liked this young piece a lot, and I patted her cheek by way of reassurance. But by then we had reached Passy Bridge, and the Swan Footpath proved inviting, so we went down the steps at that point. There, under a tree, we sat on a bench, with her perched on my knees like a well-behaved child whose grandfather is about to tell her a story. I had undone my fly-buttons, it was true, and it was also the case that she had spread out her skirts, so as to conceal my trousers and the fact that I had contrived to insert my member through the slit in her drawers. Pleasantly installed in this position, which deceives the innocent eye, we continued rocking gently to and fro. The coolness of the Seine lapped at our feet. I promised to give her the addresses of some well known artists, so that she could make a career as a model and not be 'any old tarty shopgirl', while under the warm folds of her dress and within that warmer, prettier corolla a slow, regular pulse carried us away to a powerful climax.

* * *

Maurice de Collonges was always full of surprises. And when he was not trying to seem mysterious or enigmatic and was quite straightforward, he was a riveting storyteller. He invariably had a disreputable adventure to relate or some unexpected detail or fact to report.

He it was, for example, who told me about the eccentric Baroness. She owned an isolated castle in the Ardennes apparently, where she maintained stables . . . of women. As with the notorious 'bloody Countess' Erzebeth Bathory, the women thus used were servants; about a dozen in number, they slept in stalls and upon straw. They were fed a sort of bran swill and were, naturally enough, quite naked. I decided that Maurice was a liar. But I should dearly have liked to know the Baroness and to canter after her through castle and grounds, mounted on a fine young nude.

I remember his telling me another story which he termed 'religious'. He was driving through one of the northern departments of France. Ahead of him, he saw four worthy Sisters, lending to that summery slope a distinctly funereal air. As he passed them, he noticed that they looked exhausted and were enviously eyeing the car. He also observed that they were all on the young side. He stopped, walked back to them and obligingly invited them to hop in. Eyes then raised heavenward, they sought some divine sign or permission: one solitary spotless cloud perhaps, a dove passing, the ascension of a lark. They obviously received it, and would

need to mortify themselves for being cravenly
seduced by leather seats and automobile comfort
– one of the tempting forms of contemporary
lucre. Yet they would surely pray assiduously
for the chauffeur.

They drove towards a convent that was still
some distance away. They were chatting away,
those pious little magpies of the Lord and
scarcely taking any notice of the road. When
they reached a remote cart-track, they were
astonished. Maurice stopped the car and got
out. He approached them with a pistol and
menacingly ordered them out too. They obeyed
uncomprehendingly, invoking Heaven's mercy,
then, more immediately, the man's. What did
he want from them? He lined them up facing
him. 'Take off your clothes!' And instead of
opting for death over dishonour, they did so.
He finally made them lower their sad pantaloons. From beneath the latter, some very feminine treasures were unearthed. There were
plump white stomachs, hollows patched with
black, all four sets of ungirded loins wholly
supported by firm columnar thighs. 'I just
wanted to see if there were any differences
between women and nuns. There aren't.' After
which, he climbed back behind the wheel and
drove off – leaving those virgins by vocation,
those poor parolees from God's prisons, bare-
arsed, and evidently shackled by shame to the
spot . . . And also, perhaps regretting that they
had suffered only a curtainraiser to damnation.

* * *

149

'Let's go and find the castle of the horse-women,' I said to Maurice.

'Fine,' he replied.

The very next day we set off for the Ardennes. The landscape grew flatter and flatter, until we reached a dismal pass with some sooty-looking mountains to relieve the flatness. And from there on suddenly everything grew steeper and began undulating. We were in the Ardennes. Brooks babbled vivaciously, villages became villages once more, and forests sprang thick and fast. We pushed on ever deeper through one of them. There, at the end of a long avenue of trees, stood the castle. Isolated, yes; imposingly gloomy, indeed. But my expectations were high. From his lair by the lodge railings appeared an aged codger.

'There's nothing here any more for the journalists or noseyparkers. Nothing left. The Baroness did a bunk and all the little ones were rescued. Be off with you!'

'Too late,' Maurice murmured.

I did not reply. But I suspected some fishy business. I read the newspapers regularly and they'd never mentioned this particular story. Whereas by rights it should have been headline news. Or had the whole affair been hushed up?

The journey continued, anyhow. By then we were well away and enjoying ourselves. After Belgian Luxembourg, the Duchy itself, then the Moselle country and a stay at an inn. Then

Lorraine, followed by the Vosges and a hotel high up in the pass. Strolls in the mountains, forests and lakesides. Fine fare and good wines. Yet we couldn't easily restrain our love of practical jokes, and we kept, throughout our travels, all four eyes open for any likely female gamebirds.

One Sunday in a small town, we passed a church from which the worshippers were emerging after Mass. We noticed two peasant women of that particular region and we appraised them as they were leaving. They seemed exactly right for what we had in mind. Each was a rather prematurely aged thirty or so, and each was dressed somewhat beyond her limited means. They were heading for a remote hamlet and obviously had a fair distance to walk. We decided to follow them. On the outskirts of town, I went up to them civilly. 'Ladies, my friend (I indicated the instigator of all this, Maurice) and myself had resolved to offer you some financial aid. However, in return you'll have to oblige us with a little show. We'll select a quiet glade and anyway you shan't be touched.' I went on to explain that not a finger would be laid upon their ample persons, but that they would have to strip naked and spank each other in turn. The sum we proposed paying them for this exhibition impressed them as almost indecent. They accepted with alacrity. We soon discovered – they themselves pointed it out – a pretty little dell near a waterfall, well furnished with grass and ideally quiet.

Then we were able to see these two worthy housewives undress. And each excellent materfamilias indulged in a brutal, merciless bumthrash. Indeed, they outdid each other in the berserk violence of their blows, spanking as if punishing themselves for their venality. It was a uniquely interesting spectacle, although they tried to show us as little as possible of their anatomies and remained tight-lipped throughout. We rewarded them as previously arranged, adding a small bonus.

13

During my stay in Normandy, several exhibitions were enacted for me. The Wedding Night, for example. In that one, the 'husband' was a young resident of the establishment and she wielded a dildo. Then there was the tart watching the celebrations on the Fourteenth of July. Dressed up in crinoline and split bloomers, our actress appeared, outlined against the sunlight as she opened the window; she cheered, then proceeded to do as the women of Metz had done on seeing the artillerymen emerge from the garrison after capitulating to the Prussians. Zealously, she brought herself to orgasm.

There was also the Schoolgirl Disciplined. Jeanine had been naughty. The schoolmistress was displeased and asked her to get undressed. She refused, whereupon her mistress became exceedingly vexed, bent her over, pulled down her knickers and spanked Jeanine with her bare hands. But it was clear that the mistress was not really comfortable, for she took off her own dress, seized a riding crop, and made her pupil kneel over a bench. Then she continued her instruction. The pupil seemed to lose more and more of her clothes. Finally she was naked, teacher still belabouring her and sliding the other hand – sheathed in a very long black glove – into her hirsute cleft of glistening pink.

Boasting of her journalistic ability, Irène had written a tongue-in-cheek eulogy of a romantic novel churned out by an authoress who specialised in such nonsense. The latter invited her over for a visit and Irène went along. She was astonished at her reception by the romantic novelist, who was sitting in a chair in a small office, typewriter perched on her knees – for the lady herself was stark naked. She was getting on in years but far from prudish. She told Irène that she was a fervent naturist but had no time to indulge in her hobby out of doors. Irène asked whether she found the chair rather hard. The lady suggested she sit down and try it, and when Irène did so, herself promptly sat down again on Irène's knee. What a delightful tableau!

She behaved quite unlike a romantic novelist.

It was raining very hard. Up in the mountains, the forest was never-ending. My car had broken down. I was lost, and seemed to have lost the car too. I went on walking. There had to be one house, at least, in this damp region. At last I reached the beginning of a long lane with tall fir trees on either side. Civilisation – that single house, anyway. And what would I find at the end of the lane? The chateau Meaulnes found, in the book? I walked for a good half-hour. A small manor house swathed in ivy appeared. I knocked on the door, was invited in, and entered.

A blazing fire in the hearth was the room's only illumination. Close to this fire someone was sunk deep in a huge armchair, I hazarded a guess. I went up to it and then saw that the person was a woman, scantily clad at that. She was young and strikingly, strangely beautiful. She resembled a panther or some big cat a sorcerer might have turned into a woman. Her thin shift had ridden up, and in her languid feline pose she was presenting me with a regal rump – truly untamed sensual flanks.

'I've been waiting for you a long time,' she said. *Was* she lying?

'Dry yourself. To do that properly you'll need to undress.'

No longer did I care about losing my way. Even had I suspected that for more than a fortnight afterwards I would bear the marks of her scratches all over my back and stomach.

Why had she been kept there? As punishment?

* * *

Who was this young woman with her firm yet enormous bosom exposed? The hostess with the outrageous tits, the welcomer. What a hot cunt they formed when she churned and squeezed my stiff prick between them! She had the softly tender smile of a nurse and I drenched it with all my hard ardour. What a pretty neck as it accepted my drooling libation! What fine strapping milkmaid's shoulders, and how they thrust forth her breasts, to jut and jounce in ecstasy!

In her weeds, the widow walked. She had shed her black veil edged with velvet, to reveal the wan face of her fake regret. Yet her leg thrust through the funeral hangings, her thigh set black embroidered lace trembling. She enticed you with her pain. She wept tears of desire; these seeped through the jet velvet triangular mask which plunged her motte in mourning. There it was, the mark of a previous bereavement: the loss of her childhood. She gave me nightmares but I liked to sniff past the incense and to catch the scent of her secret moistures.

Black widow with the white skin and green eyes.

The bold young woman at her mirror (title for an erotic picture) evokes, for me, the sweet perversion of voyeuristic Narcissism. Narcissism for one, when inspecting one's private parts, so-called, and in the nude of course, whether male or female. Those singular childhood discoveries!

Narcissism for two means responding, entwining, linking; proceeding via a voyeurism that involves yourself and your partner – when one sees oneself sink into velvety furred ecstasy, when she watches herself being pinned by the stiffened shaft with its twin, swollen, heavy fruits. It is a happy perversion, the secret lesson you give yourself and share with a partner in the oneiric private view, the exclusive showing of dream. Pleasure multiplied by the visual sense. The exchange of bodies and sexes. The intimate kingdom. What bliss for the man to watch himself move to and fro inside the partner, gripping and stroking feminine flesh! What bliss for the woman to observe herself being 'taken' and caressed, to look at herself quivering and bucking along a beloved body!

14

Let us move appropriately briskly to a chapter on brief loves: the passing fancies and brief encounters lasting a month, a day or an hour. What I particularly used to relish during these epidermal contacts (for they rarely involved the meeting of souls) were the preliminaries, the removal of underwear, and taking the women by that road which supposedly leads to hell after death but can be paradise on earth.

I received a letter inviting me to the 'The Impertinence Ball'. This was to be a masked ball, fancy dress optional. I did not dress up, but I did wear a mask which bore the likeness of a famour actor of the day. This was in the Vésinet, in a fine-looking mansion, more of a castle, actually. To begin with I did not spot anyone I knew, for the disguises made that very difficult. There were some people in drag, for instance, mostly women dressed as men, so it seemed.

I found a partner whose voice I did not recognise: perhaps she was purposely altering its pitch a little. Anyhow, to set the record straight, it was she who made the running. She might well have guessed my identity. She was very simply dressed: a short-sleeved bodice and a full-length beige skirt made of thick material. She wore long black gloves and a tiny hat which might have risked looking ridiculous had she herself not been so alluring. Her mask was of black velvet, worn with a black veil that hid her mouth. She danced well and we chatted brightly, paying frequent visits to the buffet to fortify ourselves with a wide range of collations and stimulants. She seemed to be chasing me rather than vice versa. Then we found ourselves alone on a terrace, perched on its balustrade gazing at the gardens and, I suppose, assessing our by now mutual desire. There was a moment of silence, after which she said:

'At one a.m. the masks come off. Those who do not wish to be recognised will be leaving before then. Would you like to know who I am – before then?'

I said I would.

She then led me along various passageways in that enormous house. Sometimes we would run across a group or a couple, but their behaviour and pastimes were generally quite innocent: some risqué conversation perhaps, or furtive, shortlived embraces. The further we walked the fewer the people, until the place suddenly seemed deserted. Like thieves, we climbed a staircase. Several of the doors on that floor were locked but we finally succeeded in finding one that opened. We went in. After which we pushed an armchair against the door. She sat down and we removed our masks simultaneously, as agreed. Then I recognised her – I had not been able to place her voice because I had not often heard it. She was the wife of my uncle Hubert the skirt-chaser; to be more specific, it was Nadine d'Evremont, Anne's sister, whom she markedly resembled. She went and leaned over the back of a chair and in so doing abruptly hoisted up her skirt, thus revealing thighs and buttocks even better developed and more voluptuous, riper than Anne's had been. I at once sported a huge erection, its volition positively devilish. I had failed to notice that during that entire evening my partner, who was also my aunt by marriage, had not been wearing any knickers.

'Since you allowed me to uncover my head, I'm also allowed to thank you by unmasking my tail.'

I was grateful to view the reverse of the medal, and in turn revealed my upright ardour, redly to the fore. Without more ado I slid readily inside her rear, taking her standing, and tucked between those generous twin globes. Her ample curves were a goddess's, they resembled the rare flanks of the wife of King Candaules, as depicted by Rubens's pupil Jordaens. Ecstasy was not slow in coming. But to be even more fully acquainted with those wonderful rotundities I needed to sit in the chair. She then sat on me, firmly and carefully pinned so as not to be thrown off during our mad gallop. The going, albeit against nature, was good. Indeed, she put not a foot wrong, as it were, and lived up and down to all my expectations. She had chosen what would best grip my rigid-grown weapon, and this I drove to the hilt in her hidden depths, which proved all sweetness and dark.

It was Chareyre, a devotee of music-hall and cabaret, who first spoke to me about the new little dancer appearing at the Théâtre du Refuge.

Her mother had been the one who introduced her to the director. She also acted as her dresser (or undresser) and waited for her after her number ended, to take her back home. There was nothing especially odd about that, but there was a certain piquancy in the fact that onstage the daughter showed most of what she had, prancing about in brassière and lace panties. She was absolutely adorable, be it noted, and remained thoroughly chaste. She danced well; her number lasted about ten minutes. But those ten minutes filled the theatre every night and made its owner a small fortune, not to mention a nice little nest-egg for the dancer, whose mother salted away her earnings, occasionally declaring that 'nothing lasts for ever, you know'. We went along to admire Isabella several nights in succession.

One evening Henri asked the mother pointblank if her daughter would care to attend a small *soirée* he was arranging at his house; she herself was of course welcome too. The girl could dance before an invited audience and the sum suggested was generous. The mother at first refused, but when the fee increased she agreed, specifying: 'Ten minutes only, mind, just like she dances here. Nothing crude or nasty.'

Somewhat frustrated to hear this, we assured her of our moral rectitude.

During this more intimate gathering, and in front of a filthy rich and toffee-nosed bunch of ladies and gentlemen, Isabella was overcome with timidity. She appeared from behind a Chinese screen and was due to dance when she was suddenly smitten with shyness or stage-fright, burying her head in her hands and bursting into tears. I thought I detected a murmur of disapproval run through the room: they would hold it against her if she did not fulfil her contract. As for myself I rushed forward, thrust her behind the screen and tried to console her, offering personally to pay her the money anyway. Finally she calmed down and prepared to try again – in her scanty black brassière and her cheeky lace knickers. She did dance, superbly. And this time the reception was overwhelming: they simply would not let her go. But she managed to make her exit, obviously appalled by the smart set. I felt sorry.

A month later I learned that Isabella had just left the Théâtre du Refuge altogether. Chareyre informed me that the pair of them had invested in a small hotel and a big bakery in a town on the Atlantic coast. The mother had adjudged that it was high time her daughter retired, since they were amply provided for, and time too for her daughter to find herself a good husband, 'not some stagedoor johnny or partygoer'. It seemed to me that lovely little Isabella, after being desired by so many men, was likely to end up a provincial lady dying of boredom and depression. I received word that Isabella wished to bid her real friends goodbye, the following Sunday morning at eleven. I turned up at her address expecting to see at least a small group of people, but I was alone. The concierge admitted me.

'I was told to expect you,' she said. 'Isabella and her mother would like you to wait for them.'

I waited. There was no longer anything much to sit upon. The room had been virtually emptied of all its furniture. I did find a small seat with a cushion and sat down. It was a long wait in that almost abandoned apartment. My every gesture and breath seemed exaggerated or resoundingly loud. Was it all a joke? At last I heard footsteps. Someone hurriedly opened the door: it was Isabella. I rose and she pecked me on the cheek.

'I'm back from Mass,' she announced.

She was still clutching her little bag that contained a missal.

'I'm exhausted, I must sit down a minute.'

She did so, then asked me to look out of the window and see if her mother was coming. The church was opposite. I stood by the window, scanning the street, but saw no one identifiable. I turned, and had the shock of my life. Isabella, who was wearing a knitted dress, had pulled up both skirt and petticoat and was sitting astride the seat, still holding her bag. Her buttocks were slightly flattened, resting on the cushion. She smiled at me and said: 'I really must pay you back.'

I thought to myself that the very wafer was still inside her stomach, and of how she had shown some audacity in going pantieless to Mass. I went over to her and she said nothing when I began feeling her bottom.

'I have to wait for mother,' she said. 'She is saying goodbye to M le Curé.'

So we waited for mother by pushing the seat up against the window, and while Isabella kept watch I officiated. Her hurdies were superb. She had her back to me and straddled me thus. She did not want to do it according to the orthodox rite, since she had vowed to remain a virgin for her future husband. I devoutly believe to this day that my prick might well have prodded the Host.

Everyone thought her an absolute angel, but I firmly felt that Isabella had something of the devil in her. I wasn't complaining.

I rang the bell where Cleo Darbois, a rising young singer lived. The door was opened by a heavy woman of indeterminate age. She also had something of a moustache; I gathered she must be Cleo's maid, chaperone, bodyguard and general fat totem.

'What do you want?'

'To see Mlle Cleo Darbois, if possible.'

'She is confined to bed. Not seeing visitors.'

'Oh but I'm sure she'll receive me.'

I was not at all sure, but I thrust my card aggressively into her hand and entered.

'I'll wait,' I added.

My confidence made her change her attitude. She climbed upstairs and plodded back, shrugging disapprovingly.

'Mademoiselle will see you.'

I satisfied myself by weighing her down with my hat, cape, scarf and cane. Then I went upstairs, my stride jaunty. Cleo greeted me with a smile. She even looked a little shy.

'Good day Monsieur Morhant,' she said.

That's true – to her, the daughter of a Metro employee and a lacemaker, I was Monsieur Morhant.

'Call me Yves, lovely Cleo.'

She blushed. It was also true that she was laid up in bed. She invited me to sit down. Twenty minutes later two steaming cups of tea, together with some fancy cakes, were brought us by the owner of a reproving moustache and a hundredweight of respectable meat. I let that moustache disappear along with the vast censorious back and, when Cleo and I were alone, began to savour the contents of the tray.

After a while she started feeling too hot. She said she had had enough of being in bed.

'You realise I've had to stay in bed a whole week? One whole week!'

I realised. And I also realised that I was seeing more and more of her thighs, which were shapely indeed. Her nightgown was riding up as she herself slid down. I also saw progressively more of her delightful bosom. Lying on, rather than in, one's sickbed can well lead to amorous delirium.

'Oh damn, it's time for my temperature. I'll have to call the dragon.'

She thought for a moment and added: 'Well, it's hardly worth the bother, the thermometer's there.'

'Would you like me to leave?'

I forced myself to take a deep breath and assume a serious expression.

'Heavens no, it's not that I want to see the back of you. You'll have to excuse me, Monsieur Yves.'

'I do and will,' I smiled, pleased to see that she meant what she said and did not wish me to go. 'And if you like, I can take your temperature myself.'

She blushed, stammering a little at that.

'If it's no trouble,' she managed finally, not looking me in the eye.

'Oh, no trouble at all, no bother.'

She lay flat on her stomach and I pulled the nightgown past her haunches. I picked up the thermometer. She let me do all this, like a trusting child. I parted her charming cheeks. Between those twins a small, still pristine eye peeped out at me. Relentlessly I poked the thermometer into it. But I did not pull back her gown, nor the sheet. I sat down to enjoy the sight of that tiny sliver of rounded glass sticking out of her arse. I waited several minutes, just like a doctor – she herself kept her head buried in the pillow - then I came back and removed the instrument. My face grave, I read out: 'Thirty seven point eight. That'll do.'

She did not answer and I continued:

'Now if you like I know another way of taking a temperature. With a different instrument, though.'

She gazed at me.

'And what if the maid came?'

'She comes only if you call her, doesn't she?'

'Yes.'

'Well then, would you care to try this other method of taking a temperature?'

'If you like!'

For one whole month Cleo became my favourite mistress. She was still comparatively innocent and I taught her as many bad habits as I could. This was why I was not taken aback, one cold morning when we were due to leave for a small country hotel, to find her still in a state of undress.

'Wait,' she said. 'I must powder my other face.'

And kneeling on a cushion she took off her flimsy nightgown and proceeded with her powder puff conscientiously to dust her buttocks.

'They were on the pale side,' she explained. 'Really they needed a bit of colour.'

After which I myself put colour into her cheeks by giving them a good hiding. We never did get to the inn. I had to console her.

Another time, in the morning again, she had not dressed because she had discovered how amusing it was to examine her naughtier geography with the aid of a hand mirror. She progressed to various contortions and exhibitions, and once again we never reached our intended destination, for I too was eager to inspect in detail, using the little mirror, all our improper contours.

One night a friend ran a short, blurry but very blue film for us. It dealt with two lesbians, servant and mistress. They were in the nude throughout, but for the servant's tiny pinafore which she flung aside with a dramatic gesture which afforded us the pleasure of encountering a shaved and distinctively deep-cleft motte. It was all quite delightful. Maid came to wake Madame, served her her tea and then, reprimanded, handed in notice and pinafore together. She needed, it appeared, considerable friendly persuasion to stay on. The narrative was simple, short and exquisitely lewd.

My good friend Henri de Chareyre, with whom I was to have something of a bone to pick, had been present at the showing. One night I met him at the Opera, and we went for a drink at the Café du Commerce. In the middle of a relaxed and somewhat intellectual discussion, he suddenly said, 'By the way, do you remember that jolly little film we saw together at Martinet's place? Well, I now know who the actresses were.'

I pricked up my ears.

'Mademoiselles Gabrielle Arroyo and Régine Rody were the frisky pair in question. They're both in the cast of a revue at the Théâtre du Refuge. We could go and see them; the show opens tonight.'

'Are you sure it was they?'

'When you see them, old man, you'll hardly believe your eyes.'

He was right. After several days of persistent invitations and deliveries of flowers, they agreed to see us in their dressing room. Then we returned each evening, showering them with gifts. They would make up in front of us, sometimes with their breasts exposed. They were far from prudish and we used to enjoy pawing those breasts and fondling those thighs, which audiences could only gaze upon from afar. Back in the theatre proper, we could savour their mincing maidenly demeanour and the bulging eyes of the male spectators.

We disclosed to them that we knew about their cinematographic talents. They had seemed both amused and anxious. We played the magnanimous gentlemen, trying not to take advantage of the situation. But one evening, when we were invited into their dressing room and we had chatted brightly as usual, those two little trollops in their white knickers and dancing pumps – like ballet students gone to seed – excited us more than ever. And, despite their vigorous if somewhat muffled protests, Henri and I pulled down their knickers and set to with a will, giving way to acts which morality condemns and performing these while standing, until ejaculation followed. At that very moment, the stage manager rapped on the door. The ladies barely had time to rearrange their knickers and get into their tutus before they themselves were onstage offering the public various pure and lyrical leaps and flights. We in their audience became wildly excited to think we alone knew what the dancers' chaste costumes contained: traces of hastily snatched carnal joys, the hurried evidence of love. We speculated as to whether front row stalls spectators might even be spattered with an occasional telltale droplet or receive some other, perhaps less palpable hint of happenings backstage.

Some people like to go off shooting; I don't care for it much. I did once accompany my friend Paul on a shoot in the Essone Valley. Near Boigneville, there are some delightful copses in almost mountainous terrain. While hopeful men with rifles crossed the nearby fields, beating for good game, the women and weaklings stayed behind with the cars. I was among the weaklings. I had breakfasted heartily, as had the bold marksmen, but that only fuelled their destructive instincts, whereas I was settling for a nap in my friend's car if it was warm enough inside. But finally I did emerge and go for a little stroll. Two hundred yards or so further on stood three empty cars. No – there was somebody inside one of them, apparently finding it as cold as I had done. It was a woman and she was not wrapped up very warmly, one had to admit. I waved pleasantly and she opened her door. 'Is there an inn anywhere close by?'

'Not for a thousand miles.'

Smiling, she stepped out. 'Brrr! My husband's a real so and so. He said, "Oh do come along darling, you won't need a coat, the inn will be warm and I'll keep coming back to see you in the car . . ." And that liar's been gone for over three hours.'

We talked for a while and then went off for a walk. Eventually we warmed up, but absorbed in our newfound friendship and our conversation, we strayed further and further afield. We reached a derelict house and wandered into its overgrown grounds.

'At least there won't be any hunters here,' I said. 'And we'll hardly be able to hear the gunshots.'

We plunged among the trees and it was better there; dead leaves crackled underfoot and the wood smelt fragrant. We were getting on well, when she suddenly asked me if she could disappear for a moment. I understood. But after a few minutes, when she had still not returned, I became anxious. Following the direction she had taken, I found her in a small glade, one foot poised on a tree trunk and quite unabashed, although her skirt was hoisted and panties lowered. What a fine, alluring dark furrow she had, surrounded by wonderfully white skin. A snowy double sorbet seemed to be on offer, as if perched atop a nice ice cream cornet comprised of lace.

'I was beginning to be afraid you wouldn't come. I was getting cold.'

'What about peeing?'

'Just an excuse.'

'A fine excuse,' I said, walking across to her. 'But how *would* you be excused?'

She gladly turned into a statuesque fountain. Standing upright again, both hemispheres bared to the breeze and in a posture of flagrant invitation, she asked for a leisurely lesson in the geography of vice.

Much later she confessed that it was the first time she had been pedicated, but also that she had found it enjoyable.

'And I was warm and glowing all over. My husband returned feeling very pleased with himself, and he remarked on what a good colour I was and how well I looked.'

Our affair continued throughout Paul's shooting trip in the Essonne Valley.

* * *

I ran into Clarisse at the Closerie des Lilas. What a surprise! We fell to talking, and to memories. Shortly after that summer together she had married an Italian count. They were staying in Paris for a few days, but her lord and master was at a business lunch. After a good two hours' chat she asked to see me the following evening with a view to our going out somewhere. I told her I would send her a message of confirmation.

This she received at five o'clock the next day, and at six I drove the car to our rendezvous as arranged. It was winter and already dark. I drove towards Belleville. We reached a dismal, squalid area with waste ground and rickety slum buildings.

'What dive are you taking me to?'

'Around us,' I replied, 'is filth. Brutal rapists. Painted sluts full of illusions and disease. The utter fatigue dulled by red wine. The enforced or wilful idleness that breeds every form of vice, and which is so often cut short by lying down one last time with old mother guillotine, as their colourful underworld slang puts it. Don't you feel that sheer, grinding poverty which weeps and groans and even clenches its fists in order not to throttle somebody?'

She was staring at me, and although the car's interior was dark, I could sense that she didn't understand what I was talking about.

'I'm going to introduce you to a young friend of mine. Because people of our class should always play patron to others less well off.'

She agreed to follow where I led. Together

we climbed the musty staircase. Children were crying, men shouting, lovers moaning in their spasms. Several storeys up I knocked on a door. Someone called out that it was not locked, and I pushed it open. The youth was lying on the bed. He looked pale, but he smiled at us. He must have thought I had come to introduce my fiancée. That was far from being the case. It was as much of a surprise for him as for Clarisse.

'Take off your clothes,' I told her.

She looked at me dumbfounded. I stood against the door.

'It's my revenge, Clarisse. You can't deny you wanted to get up to tricks with me this evening. Off with your clothes. You owe me that. As for him, he's just the age to have the illusions I had when I first knew you – and you neither deigned to write to me in Paris, nor to see me again, contrary to your promise. So off with them. For him and for me. Are you ashamed of your body?'

Then there occurred the best thing I ever saw, all under the most miserable lighting imaginable. Clarisse took off her cape and with a shy but graceful motion shed the dress beneath which (as confirmation of her ulterior motives) she was quite naked. What beauty! How magnificent she was! Her back and backside were perfect. Instead of putting on weight with age, she had if anything lost it. By witnessing this spectacle I was punishing myself, subduing a fierce desire I could not quench, for I did not even intend to lay a hand on Clarisse. The surroundings somehow set off this splendid body instead of diminishing its appeal. It was the exotic wild flower sprouting from the muck, the orchid amid, and nourished by, parasites.

'Make love to him,' I ordered finally.

She wanted to refuse and I became angry, shouting at her:

'Do you know who that bedridden boy is? Someone who will only ever have love if he pays for it or if some other miserable creature gives it him free . . . But for his paralysis he might have been the greatest violinist in the world!'

I saw Clarisse lean over him and kiss him on the forehead, more mother than lover. Then she lay down gently beside him. I went outside. When she rejoined me in the car she was weeping. She wanted to tell me something, but did not do so. I was tormented for ever afterwards by the thought that it might have been something important.

I never saw Clarisse again. But my 'young friend' informed me that she often used to send him money orders and that she was hoping to persuade her husband to bring him over to Italy. In this she was successful. To this day I wonder what the real reason for such a gesture might have been.

That apart, the above anecdote may be read as an edifying Christmas morality tale.

15

For a finale, I want a fine bouquet of images.
Those which are among the most seductive. The
ones to gleam before me and make me await the
onset of pleasure. *The supreme visions*.

Ah, those images!

The oldest one shows Mme Chartier and Mlle
Janvier. It provides a sequel to the first image
in my sexual life, my own eroticism. This photograph was rediscovered and returned to me not
so long ago, when the attic of that large house
which I inherited was being cleaned and swept.
Mlle Janvier is now a grandmother. Mme Chartier is dead. But both of them are caught for ever
in a photographic eternity, endlessly naked,
cunts exposed, and as they pose side by side
they share a curious formality, something akin
to that found in photographs of army comrades
or a pair of schoolfriends. The photograph
preserves them imperishably in my memory.
My two dear lesbians they still remain.

The next tugs at my heartstrings. My friend Paul Andrieux was married to a very attractive young woman I desired for years. I was their best friend. But the young wife was faithful as people no longer are these days. Paul died in his thirties. I found myself in charge of all the arrangements. His widow trusted me and I accompanied her home after the funeral. She wept endlessly. I told her her life was far from finished, that she could remarry and that she was still young. And it was true, she was only twenty-three and the marriage had lasted a mere four years. She had no child. She seemed inconsolable, yet we had always felt a sort of tenderness and it brought us close. She leaned against my shoulder and let herself be rocked gently in my arms. Later she found herself lying on some cushions, still in the same clothes she had worn to the cemetery, but with her skirt pulled up. Her silk underwear brought her sex into relief, the cleft clearly defined by the fineness of the material. I dwelt fondly on that vision, before consoling her with even softer and more intimate gestures.

Yet I must mention all the others too. Images of every variety, seen, lived, dreamed or invented. Immutable, eternal, ageless. Magic lantern shows composed of moments stolen from an impossible time, and which open doors into another life. Secret images that flicker, escape or elude us, sometimes fitfully revealing themselves. Perverse images that surround us, fleece us, rape us, attack us with impunity, drive us mad or beside ourselves. Dirty pictures. Shameful images. The images I have jealously kept to myself.

Meg de Vallac, as I once photographed her, would amply embody the initiatrix. The mature woman of opulent charms, who debauches young men and, why not, small boys too. With her nutcracker thighs, her vast welcoming bosom, and her sex hot as a crib in which all the little cherubs new to love can, through the flesh, be born again.

And here's the frightened virgin. What a pleasure to squeeze her young breast and feel her smooth round belly and firm thighs. She is simultaneously open to you and withdrawn. What ecstasy to teach her variations, perversions, dirty words. To inscribe upon her entire body the lore of the stiff penis, to feel her take fright and tremble.

The lady of our childhood and adolescent dreams comes next. The possessive mother. The trap-door spider, the bloodsucker which appals and attracts. Here is Venus in Furs, chastiser of men; a severe Madame of the exclusive brothel. Her breasts are full and raddled, but her thighs are big, muscular, and she has hips and haunches positively upholstered, while her sex

179

devours. Yet she is there to mete out punishment. One grovels before her, baring buttocks to ever more refined, constantly renewed torments which are always unwholesomely desired. By trying to escape from her, one only sinks ever deeper into her web. Who is lucky enough to lose himself in her and be annihilated? While she may allow you to ruin yourself, wallowing inside her, she knows all too well how crushing words can be. For she always seeks her own pleasure and to increase her power. She humiliates exquisitely.

The incestuous one. That sister of yours who is so frigid whenever her parents are about but who, when they have gone, drags you into her bedroom or begs you to scratch her back in the bath. What a difference there is in her behaviour – she becomes a snobbish little bitch when surrounded by her fashion-conscious girl-friends: how different from your knowledge of her. She might equally well be that young cousin who wants to play in the attic, or indulge in hide-and-seek in the little wood near the house. 'Show me your exclamation mark and I'll open my brackets for you.' 'Show me that hard pink granite rock and I'll let you see my fresh stream, my flowering meadow, my tiny valley.' She smells of lilacs secretly cherished, and of fields full of newmown hay.

* * *

The young woman with the sweet, gentle face, posing like an odalisque in her pure and remote nudity, is the perverse one, nonetheless – she who takes the hard homage into her mouth. It is hot, sleek, rounded, and for her it is stiffly prepared for anything, the best and worst, while come what may it twitches, pulses, ejects. As for her, she lets none of the libation run to waste. She might still technically remain a virgin, but the latter's attitudes and behaviour are no longer hers. She is already well experienced, knowing. The open, ingenuous look on that beautiful face of hers is a mask which conceals sheer greed: she wants to make you come. That is why we are drawn towards her.

Here is the slave, the sodomite humiliated, the guileless one laid low. She bends to our every whim, grovels at our feet. Offers us Sodom, gives us Gomorrah, takes us on guided tours of Babylon, surrenders herself to Baal and Beelzebub or whoever wants to make use of her body . . . That body, please note, is all too tender. She is part of every brute and villain's loot, the spoils of every mercenary's war. She is the warrior's rest.

She is here too, the naiad of apartments, the bathroom Undine. It is she who sinuously tightens around you, squeezing you into place among her ablutions. She, whose dark kelp, whose blonde algae, are wet against your hand. The fine triangular fleece becomes an aquatic plant; the pubis turns into a pearly garden when she steps out of the bath. That water one swallows while savouring her hidden grotto, the gate to the Kingdom of Thule or to Atlantis. And the lap of liquid when you take her as she crouches over pedestal or tub, or when she takes you and you lie flat upon your back. The games dripping hands play; naughty games salved by lukewarm water. Love that is truly clean and fresh, amid the scents of soap and cologne.

Is she my favourite? The lady in a hat, who has shed those black clothes which make her seem the widow of her shames. Odalisque queen. Sodom chic and elegant, haughty and triumphant Sodom. She is the snob for whom one gladly becomes a pillar of salt. The sweet panther who curls up only and always to accentuate her haunches. The socialite sodomized. That beauty encountered in the woods, correctly clad Amazon in riding clothes, or wearing an expensive ensemble from some exclusive fashion house. Always with her long discreet gloves. The hypocrite who wants to be talked about but only behind her back, and who, during sex, tries to conceal her face from you. The mysterious masked woman who looms out of the fogs of perversion, who sprawls on furs inside luxurious houses, exuding the subtlest, most suggestive perfumes. Is she my favourite?

16

On a patch of waste ground, I found a school
notebook which seemed to have been hidden
there. Leafing through it, I managed to decipher
the following:

Thursday. Mamma sent me to my room to do
my homework. I know she is having tea with
Mme Mathieu. I watch them from behind the
door in the passage. They don't take any
notice of me. When Mamma has guests, I'm
not supposed to go into the drawing-room.
Mme Mathieu has crossed her legs very high
up. I can see her thighs, right up under her
dress and she has hair between. I get all hot
and bothered. I know it's wrong to look but I
can't tear myself away. Mamma goes into the
garden to get some flowers for Mme Mathieu.
I keep looking. Mme Mathieu sees me. She
knows where I'm looking. 'What are you
looking at?'
I blush and don't answer.
'Come on, tell me!'

I remember what my friend Réné says ladies have between their legs. And I tell her. 'Your pussy.'
'Come and kiss it,' she says.

Unfortunately there the diary ends. All the same, it was promising . . .